Patrick Gloutney

Time of the Raven

Stonecroft Publishing

Create Space Edition

ISBN: 978-0-9947251-5-8

To my parents Betty Gloutney and Dr. Mark Gloutney who have always been supportive of my endeavors, from my flight training to my writing and everything in between, they have always encouraged me to continue exploring new things and have fun while doing so.

Patrick Gloutney

Books are a portal that let you experience new worlds at your own leisure, from the comfort of your own home. — Lafond 2017

Patrick Gloutney

Time of the Raven

On board the *Raven*; Bridge

Date: Unknown

Time: Unknown

Location: Time Stream

Josh Green stared at the navigation display next to his seat. He glanced at the relief helmsman, who had taken over while he plotted a new course, and then at the Captain. The Captain's face was grim. Although none of the crew onboard knew the problem except Josh and the Captain, they soon would. They were flying in a state-of-the-art aircraft designed for one purpose: to jump back and forth through time. Recent discoveries in the past few decades had shown scientists back home that time moved like a tunnel line through space. With a lot of work and technicalities that Josh didn't understand, they had built the *Raven*, a low-profile streamline aircraft with four powerful round plasma core engines mounted on supporting wings on the sides of the frame. The engines were capable of propelling the aircraft faster than anything ever built before. Fast enough to enter the purple world they were in now. The Raven had been built as a research vessel. Its mission was to collect data from the Time Stream, as they called it, which snaked its way everywhere and could bring you anywhere, at any time. The data would determine if the stream could be used as a "defensive weapon" in times of war.

The problem with so many possible options for future and past destinations was that the Time Stream was a labyrinth of glowing purple tunnels. These caused problems for the crew and ship as well. The edges of the stream were dangerous. If you didn't hit them right you would be shredded. The stream also created a field of energy preventing radio contact and making it impossible to charge anything electrical. The engine cores themselves lost 30% of their efficiency in the stream. Thankfully the ship didn't burn fuel and would never run out of power so long as the cores remained undamaged.

There was more. The stream was not meant for human travel and caused medical issues for the crew, including an increase in heavy metals such as lead and mercury in their blood. As a result, the crew all wore devices on their wrists that filtered their blood. However, these devices had a design flaw. They ran on battery power, so the ship needed to exit the Time Stream in order to charge them. The crew of the *Raven's* predecessor learned all too well the effects of not having these filters. They would be dead in an hour.

Josh checked his filter's power level, 10%. They would need to exit soon. He looked back at the NAV system. Yes, they were fast, big, advanced, cool, and living a dream but they were also indisputably...lost. The sheer number of tunnels and possibilities had overwhelmed their navigation system and rendered it useless. To add to the problem, the Time Stream led to multiple different parallel universes, making navigating by hand all that more difficult.

"Helm Master Green. A moment please," Captain Anderson requested. "What do you think?"

Josh shrugged, "We need to exit soon. But I don't know where we're going to end up."

The Captain checked his filter. Josh couldn't help but notice the red light indicating the battery was about to die. "Take control. We'll exit the next chance we get."

Josh nodded and took his seat. He swayed the ship a little feeling her controls. Everything was normal. He looked at his display. It showed engine angles, power outputs of the engines and the Time Stream, hull integrity, and much more. He watched ahead through the large windshield looking for a good spot to exit. It was going to be rough.

The Time Stream was particularly violent today, meaning they needed more force to break through. He saw his chance and took it. Aiming the ship so that her nose would cut through first, he pushed the throttles as far forward as possible. The digital gauges to his left revved high and in half a second an unimaginable roar filled Josh's ears. The ship tried to slide but Josh held it firm. He knew if he lost control it would kill them all. Then as quickly as it began it was over and they were out. The displays flickered and the proper time and date for their location could be seen on every clock.

Josh pulled back the two levers on either side of his four main throttles to slow the ship to normal flight configuration. Because the Time Stream had such different flight conditions the *Raven* had to adapt to fly in it, however the shape it had to take for Time Stream flight rendered it nothing more than a flying block barely capable of maneuvering in normal air. The changes in shape were only done with the engines. They retracted on the telescopic supporting wings and the front engines tilted back 45 degrees while the rear engines tilted forward 45 degrees forward making it appear like a flying diamond.

He turned to the Captain, "We're clear to start charging." Josh plugged his filter into his console and did a quick assessment of where they were. It was dark, but the clocks said it was day. The ship was flying normally and everything seemed to be functioning. His display suddenly turned red and showed a wall up ahead. Josh threw the Engine Pitch lever back and pulled hard on the controls. The ship slowed to a hover and Josh inched it back away from the wall. He pulled up the navigation display and his eyes widen. They were in a cave.

"Helm Master report," the Captain demanded.

"Out of the Stream sir, current flight level negative one-eight-zero. Speed zero knots." Josh reported mechanically as he tried to deduce how they had entered the Time Stream at 40 000 feet and ended up underground when they exited the Time Stream. He didn't have long to ponder as the windshield this time turned red signaling an armed threat. A display opened showing a camera view of a streak of light hitting the *Raven's* flank. The ship slid sideways and Josh grabbed the controls fighting to keep it from slamming into the tunnel wall. The weapons operator sitting at the next panel from Josh was working frantically with her controls.

"Armed contact bearing one-niner-four no lock-on."

"Arm all weapons, activate shields," the Captain ordered.

"Shields active. Still no lock-on."

"Helm Master get us out of here." Josh didn't wait for the Captain to finish his order. He jammed the Engine Pitch control forward and the ship shot ahead. He watched his display carefully guiding the large ship through the tight curving passage. He glanced momentarily at his colleague.

"Try tracking it like an object rather than a plane." He suggested as he wrestled the ship into a turn that nearly rolled her inverted. The operator, named Mira, didn't respond immediately.

"Rear weapons have a lock-on," she reported to the Captain.

"Fire." The distinctive pop of the *Raven's* lasers firing echoed through the bridge. An explosion soon followed. Mira let out a sigh. Josh did not have that luxury. The tunnel took a sharp ascending turn. There was no time to slow the ship. He had to take it at speed. He pressed hard on his yaw controls and desperately pulled his pitch/roll and engine pitch controls to try and get the ship to follow the curves of the walls. It wasn't a complete success. The shields hit the walls as the ship skidded in the turn.

"Shield integrity decreasing!" The Defense Master cautioned. Josh payed him no attention. If the ship survived the turn it would be enough. He closed his eyes, feeling every strain on the frame, every rotation of the engine and then, like a spring letting go, the ship shot out of the tunnel into a large opening, spinning like a helicopter with no tail rotor. To add to the confusion of the situation the spinning *Raven* hit something, abruptly stopping its spin. Josh stabilized the ship into a hover and then gasped when he saw what they had hit.

"My God," he heard Mira mutter. In front of them was a ship, about the same size as the *Raven*, but sleek black, perfect in every way for hiding in the dark but for the large hole in her flank the *Raven's* shields had caused. She had four large prop engines on each corner of its frame.

"What is that thing?" Josh asked. No one answered. The black aircraft slipped sideways and began to fall.

"Helm Master. Follow it," the Captain ordered. Josh complied and carefully eased the *Raven* down following the stricken black aircraft. It hit the ground hard. Its frame gave and its belly was crushed. One of the four engines broke free and fell on its side next to the dead machine. One of the massive blades from its engine stuck in the dirt perpendicular to the ground.

Mira leaned over from her chair, "How hard did we hit that thing?"

Josh stayed fixed on the sight in front of him, “Hard enough.”

Suddenly the bridge went dark.

On board the *Raven* landing craft *Eagle*

Date: May 12th, 4097

Time: 14h00

Location: Unknown

Rook watched the *Raven* as the landing craft made its way across the cave floor towards the black aircraft they had hit. He had a new respect for the Helm Master. To be able to fly a ship as big as the *Raven* through the tunnel at high speed was impressive enough, but to be able to land a computer-controlled ship as well as he had without any functioning computers, now that was something else. The *Raven* had taken a severe hit before the shields went up and it had damaged her power dispersal unit. The lights had gone out in most stations and they got lucky the computers had power as long as they did.

None of that mattered right now. The crew were fixing the problem. Rook and his team, Left Foot, Thinker, and Grease had been ordered to investigate the ship the *Raven* had brought down. Their landing craft stopped and they all climbed out. They had collectively decided to leave the craft behind for a quick getaway should it be needed. No one else was in the landing craft but his team so they weren't leaving anyone at risk by leaving it behind for the moment. As they approached the black aircraft the force of its impact became more evident. Ridges of sand rose up around its beaten frame and the frame itself was cracked and torn.

Grease unsnapped his pistol. "Helm Master did a number on this thing."

Rook nodded. "Glad we had the shields on." They moved into the gash the *Raven* had caused. There were no lights inside aside from the small light beams their flashlights threw. They walked for what seemed like hours through a maze of hallways. There were no off shooting pathways just the one they were on, but it twisted and turned like the intestines of a mammal. Every once in a while the frame would groan as a new part collapsed. It seemed the frame of this ship was falling apart faster every second. Rook was waiting for the section they were in to fall on them.

Eventually they encountered an obstacle. A wall, or at least Rook thought it was a wall. He ran his flashlight over it. It looked to be a sort of semi-transparent organic membrane with something dark red behind it. Rook half expected it to start glowing.

He looked back the way they had come, "Any ideas?"

Left Foot poked the membrane with his gun, "We could cut it."

Grease didn't hesitate. He drew his blade and moved to the membrane. His arm went up and Thinker grabbed it. "Wait! What if it's like the *Raven's* engines?"

Rook frowned. If Thinker's notion was right, and he was rarely wrong, behind that membrane could be a substance that could eat through a human being faster than Rook's cousin could devour a hot dog. Rook ran his light across the ceiling looking for a way around this thing. He didn't need to wait long as the frame produced a loud groan and something close collapsed. The membrane in front of them moved then stretched towards them.

Rook instantly knew what was coming next, "Run!" The order was barely out of his mouth when the membrane broke sending gallons of a slime like substance toward them. It took every team member off guard and they were swept down the hallway. Rook tumbled down the hallways, bouncing left and right till eventually he fell through a hole in the ship's hull. He hit the sand with a thud. He tried to run but the slime made movement impossible. He looked around but his teammates were nowhere to be seen. The ship beside him let out another groan as it completely collapsed. The flank bent outwards till it shattered. Pieces of ribbing flew out leaving marks like the teeth of an animal. The engine off to Rook's left began to fall. He could see the massive prop falling towards him. He tried to run but he only slipped and fell on his face. Before he could move again the prop impaled him through his back.

On board the *Raven*; Bridge

Date: May 12th, 4097

Time: 16h09

Location: Unknown

"Eagle come in," the radio operator shouted. Josh watched transfixed as the aircraft they had hit disintegrated before them, turning into nothing but sand. He glanced at Mira who was equally amazed by the decaying ship. Josh ran his hands over the controls, thinking about if that were the *Raven*. It was odd but he couldn't imagine what the crew of that ship must be going through. Watching your ship fall apart would be like watching your house burn to the ground.

The Captain's hand rested on Josh's shoulder. "Come with me." Josh obeyed and was led to the Captain's private cabin. Most of the crew lived in large rooms out of bunks called barracks. There were only a few cabins onboard and they were reserved for the Captain, First Officer, Engine Master, Helm Master, Weapons Master, Defense Master, and others that held the ship's Master positions. They weren't magnificent, just simple white rooms with a bunk, table, and screen to display anything of importance to the reident. Josh for example had a live feed of everything ranging from engine pitch to air speed.

The Captain took a seat on his bunk. "What are the chances that happens to the *Raven*?"

Josh searched for an answer, “I don't know. I'm not really the one to ask sir. The mechanics would know better than I would.”

“I am asking you. You know this ship and her limits better than anyone. Do you think that could happen?”

“I don't see how. Unless it's something in the air or ground causing it.” Josh replied.

The Captain nodded, “Get some rest. Computers should be up and running by the morning and I want us out of here as soon as possible.”

“Forgive me, but you know what that means right?”

The Captain nodded again, “Getting up high.”

Josh ran his hands through his hair, “When the computers are running again could I get the radar to give me as detailed a map as possible? Maybe we will be able to find a way out of these tunnels.”

“You'll have it.” the Captain assured.

Josh saluted the man and turned to leave. He stopped at the door. “Why the sudden interest in me?”

The Captain raised an eye brow, “You're my Helm Master.”

“This is a conversation normally discussed by the Captain and his First Officer, not with a Helm Master.” Josh pushed.

“You really want to know?” The Captain asked. Josh nodded. “I think you’re the only one who can get us home.”

On board the *Raven*; Cargo Bay One

Date: May 12th, 4097

Time: 21h00

Location: Unknown

The large steel box slid down the rail and locked into place with a satisfying clank. It was then carried by crane to the end of the cargo bay where it would be unloaded and refilled. Doug loved to watch his command work. It ran like a well-oiled machine. So much so, that even though Doug was the *Raven*'s Load Master, there wasn't much he needed to do. Most of the day he spent walking around and supervising, making a few minor corrections here and there, or filling out the paper work everyone hated.

He looked down at his tablet, happy the computer system was back up and running. "Container one-niner-five needs to be moved so we can balance," he instructed. They had to do a bit of shifting so the *Raven* would remain balanced after the loss of one of her landing crafts. With nothing much more for Doug to do he glanced out a port hole. What he saw made him drop his tablet. In the distance was a set of lights making its way toward the *Raven*.

He grabbed his communicator. "Unknown craft approaching the stern. All we got is lights."

There were a few seconds of silence before the Captain replied, "Computer says it's the *Eagle*. Let it in, but treat it as hostile. We don't know what's out there."

Doug agreed and soon had his entire work force armed and ready. They lowered the ramp and formed two lines down either side of it. The *Eagle* was armed so Doug was ready to raise the ramp at the slightest hint of trouble. Thankfully none presented itself. The craft hovered in, just like it was supposed to, and parked in its usual spot. The workers circled the craft, guns raised as more armed guards joined the party. Doug typed the access code into the door's keypad and it slid open. No one had to wait long before an injured Rook came limping out. A collective sigh of relief was let out by everyone.

Doug rushed to help the man, taking note that no others were in the landing craft, "You're supposed to be dead man."

"Guess I'm a ghost then," Rook replied weakly.

Doug helped Rook to a seat and grabbed his radio, "Medical emergency in cargo bay one."

"*Eagle's* engine was dead," Rook said.

"Don't worry about that right now. We'll get you fixed up, Where's the rest of your team?" Doug replied. Rook didn't answer.

The *Raven*'s medical crew came rushing in and brought the man to the sick bay. The Captain, Doug and for some reason the Helm Master were there with him. They cut his uniform off to get at the injury and Doug gasped when he saw the wound. It was a huge gash in his back, it looked like he should have been cut in half, yet the wound didn't bleed.

"What happened to you Rook?" the Captain asked.

"We got caught in the ship's belly when it went down. I got lucky I guess and got out."

"Lucky's an understatement, my young lad. You should be dead with a wound like that," the Doctor said. There were murmurs of agreement around the room. The officers all left Rook and the Doctor and met outside.

"What do you think?" the Captain asked.

"I agree with the Doctor, he should be dead." Doug replied.

"Josh?" the Captain prompted.

"I don't like his story. We took out most of the ship's belly when we hit and the rest was destroyed in the impact. How do you get caught in something that isn't there?" the Helm Master answered.

"Are you saying he's lying?" Doug accused defensively.

"I'm saying it doesn't add up. I mean it's not uncommon for people to mix up a situation like that. Especially with a wound like that."

"I don't like it. Why wait hours to return if you're hurt that bad?" the Captain asked.

"Maybe he couldn't get to the landing craft quickly. He said something about the engine not working." Doug suggested, feeling anger begin to well up inside him. Rook was his friend and he didn't like what the Helm Master and Captain where insinuating.

The Captain nodded. "Look in to that will you? I doubt we have cause for concern but I'd rather be safe. That will be all gentlemen. Thank you."

On board the *Raven*; Helm Master Cabin

Date: May 12th, 4097

Time: 21h30

Location: Unknown

The doors to Josh's cabin slid open and he dragged himself into the darkness. He was exhausted, but also perplexed. Not only did Rook's story not add up but neither did his injuries. From the look of the wounds the man should have died with that ship. To make matters worse, the Captain wanted his opinion on the matter. He had no qualifications in the medical field and certainly wasn't a leader. Josh plunked himself on his bunk to be thrown off by a startled Mira.

"Holy crap Josh. You scared me half to death."

"I scared you? What are *you* doing in *my* cabin?" Josh shot back, though he knew the answer. He dropped his voice, "You know this is against the rules."

Mira sat up and turned the bed light on, "Never stopped you before."

Josh shifted, "We need to follow the rules. Mira." There was a long moment of dead air before Mira spoke again.

"Are we lost Josh?"

Josh nodded, "The complexity of the Time Stream overwhelmed the navigation system. I haven't figured out a way to navigate manually yet."

Mira moved behind Josh and began to massage his shoulders. He let out a contented sigh, “To make things worse the Captain is relying on me to get us home.”

Mira stifled a laugh, “You are the Helm Master.”

“And you're the Weapons Master, yet you're not responsible for bringing a whole ship home safely.”

Mira stopped her massage, “No, you're right. I only shoot the guys on your ass so you can keep running.”

“Mira I didn't mean—”

Mira waved a dismissive hand, “You may have to bring the *Raven* home but I'm the one that hits the button to end another person's life. Don't ever think you have it worse because I can guarantee that others have it worse then you. Just like others have it worse than me.”

Josh's mind instantly went to Rook. He had lost his entire team and nearly been killed, and here Josh was thinking he had the worst of it all, and questioning the man's accounts of what had happened. Rook had been there, Josh hadn't, and it was wrong of Josh to think he could judge the situation from the outside.

He gave Mira a hug, “You okay?”

“Fine. I just don't like pulling the trigger.”

"You picked a bad position then," Josh joked. It got a smile from Mira.

"It was the only officer position left."

"Think of it this way. Whenever you kill that one enemy, you save all the lives on board the *Raven*. That guy you got today took one shot at us and nearly knocked us out of the sky. If he had taken another, there's no telling what might have happened. You made sure that we didn't have to find out."

On board the *Raven*; Bridge

Date: May 13th, 4097

Time: 06h00

Location: Unknown

The console came to life in a swirl of colours. Everything was displayed for Josh, just the way he wanted. He was glad that the computer system hadn't been restored to its default setting as it took him forever to find a configuration that he liked. He took the controls and gently eased the *Raven* off the cave floor. To him all felt normal.

"Shields are now active," the Defense Master reported. The Captain had ordered the shields and weapons to be armed and ready in case they got another sneak attack. Josh knew what he was thinking. There was no way that the home base of the two craft they had seen so far hadn't been notified of the presence of a ship as big as the *Raven*. He was waiting for the reinforcements. Thankfully the *Raven's* radar had been able to paint a very clear picture of the tunnel system around them and the navigation system had been able to pick a path that was most likely to lead them out. Unfortunately, the labyrinth of tunnels was immense and the radar map didn't show an end. As a result, Josh flew slowly but kept the engines ready for another evasive dash to escape an attack.

Josh glanced at Mira as he guided the *Raven* through the tunnel the navigation system had picked. She looked normal. There was no sign that she regretted her position. She looked completely ready to pull that trigger once again should someone threaten the *Raven*.

They flew with little conversation on the bridge for most of the day till the radar showed what might have been the end of the tunnel system. Josh pushed the *Raven* faster as they rounded the last corner and saw the light. A cheer rose from the bridge crew. They were out. Josh smiled but just as they cleared the entrance to the outside world, a wave hit the *Raven* broad side. Her rear left engine hit water and flamed out. Josh jammed his yaw controls and steadied the ship but the lost engine proved a challenge. The *Raven* wanted to fall with only three of her four corners supported. Josh was so obsessed with getting the missing engine going that he didn't notice the sight that had captivated the rest of the bridge crew. When he did, he partially jumped out of his seat. Setting aside the fact there was nothing but a deep purple liquid in sight, there were hundreds of hovering craft with large guns mounted on them, multiple floating vessels and there were three large ships like the one they had hit. The computer displayed the redundant information identifying them all as threats.

"Helm Master," the Captain called.

"Sir?"

"Get us out of here."

Josh responded quickly by jamming his throttles forward. He saw no value in going up, they would expect that, instead he headed right for the fleet of ships. It worked. They scattered like flies. Josh could see Mira working to track as many targets as possible. No one had fired yet, so neither would she. Josh's own display showed the small aircraft had regrouped and was now pursuing the *Raven.* He needed to get high and fast so he could enter the Time Stream, but if he didn't play this right, they might not be able to get the speed they needed in time. A flash of light flew past the *Raven* as a pursuer's shot missed. Knowing Mira now had the right to shoot back, he swung the ship around and positioned it for a shot, but Mira never fired.

"Weapons Master!" the Captain called. Still the *Raven* never fired. A shot from the enemy hit the *Raven's* shields and erupted in a vibrant display of colors.

"Shields holding at full strength," the Defense Master reported.

The Captain reached around Mira and fired the *Raven's* lasers. Several of the approaching craft exploded and the rest scattered. Josh let the *Raven* out of her hover and sent her into a spinning vertical climb. It quickly climbed to 40,000 feet. Josh could see the large ships of the enemy climbing to meet up with them. The smaller crafts apparently couldn't make the trip as they stayed low. Josh pushed the engine pitch control forward and the *Raven* jolted onwards. He slid the levers into place to configure the ship for Time Stream flight and waited for the airspeed.

A shot from the enemy hit them broadside causing the *Raven* to spin out of control. Josh grappled with the controls, trying desperately to regain the ship's stability. The problem was, to do this he would have to change the ship back to a normal flight configuration. Then he thought of something. His airspeed was almost enough to break into the Time Stream. He let go of the controls and the *Raven's* spin increased in violence, but so did her airspeed. Just before they slammed into another one of the large enemy ships, a flash of purple light erupted and they were in the Time Stream.

On board the *Raven*; Bridge

Date: Unknown

Time: Unknown

Location: Time Stream

The *Raven's* spin didn't stop when she entered the Time Stream. Josh pumped the yaw controls, desperate to prevent her from hitting the side walls. Finally, he got the ship into a predictable and manageable swaying pattern, but she was nowhere near stable. He kept working the controls, slowly flattening the ships sways. Unfortunately, the Time Stream had other plans; up ahead it split, both options sharp turns. Josh broadsided the *Raven* into the left split and then worked the engine pitch controls to keep the ship in its turn. An ear-splitting screech filled the bridge as one of the Raven's engines grabbed the side of the Time Stream. The ship shuddered, but held. Josh's hands moved from control to control automatically knowing what needed to be done and when to do it. As the Time Stream narrowed, he brought the ship back to a normal flight position and then, as if he had planned it, found its sweet spot; the one position in the Stream where the force of the engines on the Stream's walls kept the ship locked in the center and required very little attention from Josh. He let go of the *Raven's* controls and leaned back. Sweat covered his brow and the controls glowed in the purple light of the Time Stream, but he was content that he had done his job.

The stability in the bridge didn't last long as the Captain's stern voice rang out, "Weapons Master."

Every eye on the bridge turned to Mira, "Sir?"

"Explain your actions."

Mira hid her shaking hands as she turned to face the Captain, "I didn't like the shot."

"Your Helm Master set you up perfectly for an offensive. You had nothing to do but push a button, yet I had to intervene," the Captain pushed.

"I have no suitable explanation, sir," Mira stated plainly.

The Captain nodded, "Your hesitation put the entire ship and crew in danger. You are dismissed."

Mira saluted and left. Josh wanted to follow to comfort her. He knew exactly what had happened but it would look really bad if he moved. Their relationship was already against the rules and the crew didn't need anything to add to their current predicament.

"Helm Master? Can the ship make do without you?" the Captain asked. Josh nodded his response, too much in shock to respond properly. "Good. Number one."

Josh followed the Captain out of the bridge and into an elevator, "What is this about?" Fear that the Captain had discovered his relationship with Mira began to creep inside him.

The Captain made a selection on the elevator panel, "It's about the landing party we sent out to that ship," The Captain explained. "Doug checked the *Eagle*. Then he had the Engine Master look it over. There was nothing wrong with her engine. Means Rook lied about its engine trouble. He had no reason to not immediately return from that ship after it collapsed. We're going to sick bay to check in with the Doctor about his condition." The elevator stopped and they were soon in the sick bay of the ship. The white walls seemed uncomfortably white for Josh. He had never liked the sick bay. He always thought of it like he thought of the dentist.

"What do you have for me Doctor?" the Captain called. The Doctor came around the corner from his office, pushing his glasses farther up his nose.

"Ah, Captain. You want to know about Security Officer Rook, correct?" he asked. The Captain nodded. "Helm Master? Here for the checkup you missed last week?" The Captain gave Josh a look.

"Not right now, I'm afraid," Josh stated.

"Too bad. I do enjoy it when we talk," the Doctor said, "This man can tell you almost anything about the ship. Her controls, flight limits. He once even speculated on how the ship would fly underwater! Imagine that!"

"That's all very interesting. But could you show me your findings about Rook?" the Captain asked.

The Doctor nodded, "My mistake. The man should be dead. But he isn't. The injury to his back was severe at best. It's a miracle that he wasn't cut in two. The peculiar thing though is that none of his internal organs appear to have been damaged," the Doctor opened photos on the wall-mounted display showing the wound, "I had considered that maybe the injury was two glancing blows but if you look at the wounds and the tissue surrounding, it is pushed in on one side and pushed out on the other leading me to believe that the object passed through Rook. However, once again, none of his internal organs were damaged. I'm at a complete loss for an explanation."

"Did you determine what made the wound?" the Captain asked.

The Doctor fiddled with the screen and pulled up a 3D model. "This is my best guess as what it looks like, but I can't for the life of me identify it."

Josh moved closer to the image. It looked familiar. "Could I have a piece of paper?" he asked.

The Doctor handed him one, "What are you thinking of, young man?"

"The shape looks familiar but I can't put my figure on it."

"Could it be a weapon used where we just exited?" the Captain proposed.

"I don't think so..." Josh let himself trail off as he completed his drawing. He was right. He handed the drawing to the Captain, "It's a prop."

"You're sure?"

"Look at the shape."

"Looks like a wing," the Doctor commented.

"Except the camber is wrong. This wing wouldn't support an aircraft, it would however, create thrust rather effectively."

"What are you proposing?" the Captain inquired.

"It's going to sound crazy but I think Rook was impaled on one of the large props of that ship he was sent to inspect." Josh explained.

"It would match my findings. There's something else too. I found this on his clothing." The Doctor held up a vial of reddish liquid. "It's organic but I don't know what it's from." The Captain looked to Josh.

He wracked his brain for an answer, ignoring the fact that he was grossly underqualified for such an inquiry, but found nothing. "I hate to suggest this but could it be possible that Rook isn't Rook? What if he's some creature from the world we just came from that can mimic others?"

"So it would mimic only the external injuries," the Captain rubbed his forehead.

"And none of the internal ones. That's genius, boy!" the Doctor chimed in.

The Captain grabbed his radio. "Security Command? You are hereby authorized to detain Rook until further notice, using any non-lethal force necessary." He then turned to the Doctor and Josh, "I hope to God you're wrong."

On board the *Raven*; Security Command

Date: Unknown

Time: Unknown

Location: Time Stream

"Are we really going to arrest Rook?" one of the men on Alt's team, nicknamed Sharp Shooter, asked.

"We have our orders." Alt responded. If he was honest with himself he didn't want to do this. Rook was part of their unit, he was family and it felt like a betrayal for the Captain to have ordered the arrest of one of their own.

"You don't like them?" the Security Master asked.

Alt slid the magazine into his gun, "No, but I'll follow them."

"Good man. Now bring him home alive. Hopefully we can sort out whatever mess he's gotten himself into." With that the team was off, making its way to the recovery center onboard. Alt knocked, but there was no answer. Alt overrode the lock and they moved in. It was dark and the only light was from their flash light beams and the eerie purple glow of the Time Stream coming in from the port hole. A shot, followed by a scream, ripped through the silent compartment. Alt rushed into an adjoining recovery room to see a figure run further into the recovery center. His team followed while he dropped next to Sharp Shooter's inert body. Gun shots erupted next door as Alt failed to find a pulse on his fallen friend. Another shot sent a momentary flash of light into the room and Alt jumped. Sharp Shooter had a three-foot piece of metal sticking out of his chest. Alt left the body and moved to the other room to help the others. He was no help. As he entered the room he was jumped and held in a firm grip. The only thing was, his captor didn't feel human. It felt cold and metal like with a coating of slime-like substance.

"Drop your weapons!" Rook's voice shouted. A gun rested against Alt's temple. To his surprise the gun looked as though it was part of an arm. He was too stunned to do anything. His two remaining men lowered their weapons and Rook shot one. The other dove for cover but Rook wasn't letting him get away. He threw Alt to the floor and approached the hiding team member. Alt had to act fast. By now alarms were ringing, signaling the rest of the crew to the gun shots. It wouldn't be long before reinforcements arrived, but it might still be too long. Alt didn't hesitate. He lunged for Rook and jammed him against a door. The door slid open and they fell into the hall. Alt recovered and retreated back into the room, forgetting that he was now giving this monster easy access to the ship. Rook however didn't give up, he lunged for Alt, but as the door slid shut, it caught his gun/hand and sliced it clean off. Alt fixed his light on the disembodied arm. The flesh melded perfectly to form a .45 caliber semi-automatic pistol with no trigger. It was by far the strangest thing Alt had ever seen. Then the arm started to melt. It formed a puddle of sliver metallic liquid and, to make things weirder, retreated under the door. Alt carefully slide the door open and moved out to try and find Rook. He was gone.

Alt grabbed his radio, "We lost him."

On board the *Raven*; Bridge

Date: Unknown

Time: Unknown

Location: Time Stream

The sound of gunshots echoed through the *Raven's* bridge. Josh had hoped that Rook would go easily and this whole thing would be one big misunderstanding, but the crashing and yelling coming over the security team's monitoring system made it clear that wasn't going to be the case. He did a quick check of his instruments and noticed that the number four engine's temperature was fluctuating. Josh ran a diagnostic but got inconclusive results. His concern grew as he realized it was the engine that had hit the Time Stream's wall. He was about to notify the Captain when another shriek of pain erupted from the *Raven's* speakers. Josh looked to the front to see the head cam view of the security team. What he saw made his gut turn, an arm lay on the ground, severed by one of the *Raven's* doors.

What the heck? he asked himself as the arm melted and slid under the door. Josh looked to the Captain who had been talking with the First Officer.

His face was grey as he grabbed the PA microphone. “Attention all crew members the *Raven* is now in lock down, effective immediately.” The Captain replaced the microphone and turned back to the First Officer. “Sound the alarm. Authentication code niner-zero-alpha-delta-four.” Within seconds, a low monotone alarm sounded and all the doors to the bridge sealed. Additionally, the doors were covered by gates on the inside, and a second door on the hallway side. This combination would be repeated across the entire ship. The problem was that this situation was never truly anticipated. The *Raven* was a nearly impenetrable fortress from the outside, but it was not designed to be defended against an internal attack. If Rook was inside a cabin he would be trapped, but if he was in the hallways, he could go anywhere and hide, making finding him all that more difficult.

"I want search teams moving immediately. We need to find and neutralize Rook," the Captain explained over the phone to the Security Command.

"Sir?"

"Yes Helm Master?"

"Does Rook have access codes for the doors?" Josh asked.

The Captain paused, then put the phone back to his ear, "I want all access codes for the doors changed...I don't care! Get it done! Quick!" With that he hung up the phone. "Thank you Helm Master."

"There is something else—" Before Josh could finish a high-pitched alarm sounded from his console.

No! he thought to himself as he bolted to his seat. Much as he expected, the number four engine failed as he took his seat. The rear starboard corner of the ship fell and hit the Time Stream wall. Josh pulled the engine pitch controls and managed to level the *Raven* but he wasn't sure how long it would hold. The sweet spot the *Raven* was in had disappeared. That along with the engine power decreasing made controlling the ship all that more difficult.

"Helm Master report," the Captain demanded.

"Number four engine failure. Ship stable for now but won't make a turn," Josh reported.

"We have movement in engine room four," a Security Officer stated.

Josh continued his wrestling with the *Raven*, "Sir, if that's Rook, he could blow the whole ship."

There was no immediate response from the Captain but when he did respond it was not what Josh wanted to hear. "Dispatch security to engine room four. Helm Master. keep her steady."

"Sir! We need to exit now," Josh protested.

"It is easier to contain him if we're in the Stream," the Captain responded.

"Won't matter if we're all dead!" Josh shot back, suddenly aware of how much he was over stepping his bounds.

Again, there was no immediate response. “How long can you hold her?”

“Two minutes max. Engine temps are rising and efficiency is decreasing. We wait any longer and we won’t have the speed to get out or stay up.”

“Find us a spot to exit,” was all the Captain said. Josh shifted his attention to the instruments. His remaining engines were almost at their limits trying to hold the *Raven*. He glanced at the quick display for the navigation system. He had no idea where they would come out. The gunshot alarm sounded and displayed that the shots were coming from inside engine room four. At that moment, Josh saw a spot to exit. He let the pitch controls go and pushed the *Raven’s* nose down. A flash of light and they were out diving towards the ground. Josh pulled the *Raven* up and tried to level her, but the lost engine proved too much. The *Raven* rolled and dove again. Josh tried, in desperation, to restart the failed engine and to his surprise it started. With it now running, he leveled the ship and turned his attention to the front. He saw Rook jumping one of the security members. Without hesitating, Josh rolled the *Raven.*

On board the *Raven*; Engine compartment four

Date: July 11, 1503

Time: 11:00 zulu

Location: 69.918364°N 70.9865°W

Alt raised his arms as Rook came at him, a knife-like feature making up his right arm pointed at Alt's chest. Then suddenly gravity shifted, as if the *Raven* had rolled onto her back and now Alt was falling onto Rook. He didn't hesitate. He drew a knife and plunged it into the man's chest as they hit the ceiling of the engine compartment. The *Raven* shifted again and they slid to a wall, where Alt withdrew his blade. He got his footing and raised his blade defensively.

Rook just smirked. "Just like I thought."

Alt looked to his blade. It was gone from the hilt down, as if an acid had eaten the metal blade away. Before Alt could even react to this discovery, Rook slashed his leg. He cut him deep to the bone. Rook slashed again at Alt's arm. He missed as the *Raven* suddenly righted herself, sending them crashing to the floor.

Alt recovered as best he could but had a hard time keeping his balance. The pain in his leg was excruciating but to his surprise the *Raven's* deck kept shifting every time he was about to fall, keeping him steady and making difficult the approach of the creature that had once been Rook.

What the hell does he mean? Alt questioned as he quickly radioed for help. He started to fall and grabbed a pipe for support when he saw his gun laying on the floor. He lunged for it. He got it and fired three shots into the creature. The shots passed right through and punctured a pipe behind him. The creature didn't bleed, the wounds healed as quickly as they were inflicted. Alt desperately tried to find a way to win but it was becoming apparent he wasn't going to.

"Watch what you're shooting at. Bullets and plasma cores don't mix well," the Engine Master said through his ear piece.

"You're not the one that has to—" the monster grabbed Alt and slammed him into a wall, bursting yet another pipe. Alt felt a sharp pain in his back coupled with a freezing cold liquid running down his arm. The creature dropped him and he fell like a rag doll. Then the creature started walking away. Alt shifted so he could see what he had hit. A clear steaming liquid was falling on his legs, but he couldn't feel anything. He looked at the pipe; it was a cooling pipe for the engine's core. He hauled himself up with considerable effort and plenty of painful protest from his back.

He fired again at the monster's back, "Where you going? I'm still alive. Come and finish the job, you miserable piece of shit."

Rook turned, "You can't win. Your host will be mine. Give up now. Save us all the effort,"

Host? Alt thought, *He thinks the Raven's alive!* "You'll never take it. It killed you once, it will do it again!" Alt hollered playing along, "You're just a pathetic, worthless, useless carcass!" Alt's comments had the desired effect. The creature lunged at him. Alt pulled with all his might and ripped the damaged pipe from the wall, spraying the monster with its pressurized contents. A hand shot from the cloud of fog and stopped just a fraction of an inch from Alt's neck. Alt let himself fall to the floor as the super cooled liquid froze his assailant and alarm lights flashed.

On board the *Raven*; Engine compartment four

Date: Unknown

Time: Unknown

Location: Time Stream

Josh couldn't get over what he was seeing. After reentering the Time Stream the Captain requested Josh's presence as he went to see what was once Rook. Though Josh could have done without the damage to the *Raven*, he had to admit that the security officer had been most effective in disabling his opponent. Rook, no not Rook, the creature stood, completely frozen through, one arm stretched unnaturally long and reddish in color, looked like a rusting metal statue, while the face was contorted in what looked like a mixture of pain and anger.

"I've never seeing anything like it," the Doctor stated from behind Josh, "I mean, it looks almost as though he's made of mercury or something. Very fascinating."

"How's Alt?" the Captain asked. Josh smiled. It never ceased to amaze him how the Captain could remember every crew member's first name. On board, it wasn't so much a sign of respect or disrespect if the Captain called you by your first name, but if he called you by your rank, he had the utmost respect for you.

"The poor lad will never walk again. That pipe, it looks like his spine was crushed on it. It severed the young boy's spinal cord. He'll be paralyzed from the waist down. It's a good thing his blood filter escaped injury. If that wasn't enough the fluid in the pipe leaked onto his leg. It reminds me of a case back home. A man stranded himself in a snow storm, he had the worst—"

The Captain discreetly rolled his eyes, "Doc, Alt please."

"The fluid would have caused instant freezing of the flesh," Josh interjected.

The Doctor adjusted his glasses, "Yes. It did. In fact, his legs were ready to shatter when I got to him. We had a hell of a time getting him to sick bay."

"What did he spray Rook with?" the Captain inquired.

Josh again spoke before the Doctor could, "They're cooling lines for the engine. It's a feeding line so the coolant is super cooled and then sent to the core where it would be heated and sent for cooling."

The Doctor smiled, "See, not even his department and he knows the ship better than us."

Josh retreated slightly, "Sorry. I shouldn't have cut you off."

The Captain chuckled, "Don't be. I doubt the Doctor would have known the answer anyway." Josh nodded and fully retreated.

"Helm Master," the Doctor called, "Alt would like to speak to you." This got a raised eyebrow from the Captain.

"I best not keep him waiting then. Sir." Josh saluted, and left.

Once in sick bay Josh quickly found Alt. He was covered in white bandages from his toes to the end of his arms. His face showed evidence of extreme freezer burn from the liquid he had used as a weapon.

The battered man looked at Josh. His eyes gave nothing away, "I take it you did fine without that engine."

Josh nodded slowly, "I did. Good thinking with the cooling line." Alt said nothing. "You wanted to speak with me."

Alt nodded, "I need to thank you. You changed the playing field to my advantage there. It was a much needed helping hand."

"Some good I did you." Josh motioned to the man's legs.

"Could be worse. Without your help, I could be dead right now."

There were a few moments of tense silence. Josh could tell there was something else. "What's on your mind?"

"It's going to sound crazy. But some of the things it said..."

"Try me. Can't be crazier than a stretching creature," Josh encouraged.

"It called the *Raven* our host. Said it was going to take *our* host," Alt explained.

Josh sat in a chair. *What the heck does that mean?*

"Are you thinking what I'm thinking?" Alt asked.

"What are you thinking?"

"It's host was the ship we sent Rook and his landing party out to. The ship the *Raven* hit."

On board the *Raven*; Crew Quarters, Female Compartment

Date: Unknown

Time: Unknown

Location: Time Stream

Josh adjusted the strap on his blood filter and checked its battery. During their brief exit from the Time Stream they were able to re-charge the Blood Filters leaving them with plenty of power when Josh re-entered the ship. The *Raven* could fly in the Time Stream for a good couple of days before they would need to exit again.

He walked down the hallway on his way to check on Mira. He couldn't imagine what it would have felt like to be dismissed the way she had been. He was hoping to avoid running into anyone but that hope was rendered moot as he rounded the corner.

"Helm Master?" Female Security Officer Cranston asked, "What are you doing here?"

Josh once again played with the strap on his blood filter, "I just came to check in on my partner."

Cranston raised an eyebrow as Josh realized he had not chosen the best words. "Your partner?"

Josh nodded, "Yes. The Weapons Master and I work as a team on the bridge. In an offensive, I position the ship so she has the best angle for a shot and in a defensive move she makes sure I have room to get away," Josh stopped himself, realizing he was over justifying his presence in the female quarters, "She had a bad day on the bridge today and I wanted to make sure she was okay." There was no response from the officer. "Is that a problem?"

"No sir. Just never considered two Masters as partners."

Now it was Josh's turn to raise an eyebrow, "Really? Why would that be?"

"All the other Master are so protective of their stations. They seem...stand offish."

"They don't have the lives of an entire ship on their shoulders like Mi—the Weapons Master and I." Josh stated.

"Sorry to bother you sir. Tell Mira I hope she's feeling okay."

Josh agreed and made his way to Mira's cabin, "Mira? It's me. Open up."

The door slid open and Mira pulled him in just as it shut, "What are you doing here? You trying to get us caught?"

Josh pulled his wrist from her grip, "Nice to see you too."

Mira's expression softened, "Sorry Josh. I'm a little stressed right now."

"I can imagine. You doing okay?"

Mira nodded, "I just hope that the Captain will give me another chance."

Josh chewed on his thoughts. He needed to ask the next question but dreaded it, "Mira, can I count on you to fire next time?"

Mira looked at him, "Are you questioning my competency?"

"You did make the Captain fire the ship's weapons."

"I can't believe you of all people would question me!"

Josh didn't back down, "Can I count on you? Will you fire? If you can't answer that question then you shouldn't be in the position of Weapons Master."

Mira gave him a look of disgust, "I hate it when you're right." There was a pause before she continued, "I will. I just have to think like you."

Josh ran his hand through his short hair, "What is that supposed to mean?"

Mira placed a hand on his chest, "I need to take every threat to the ship personally."

"I do not—"

"Really? You just chewed me out because I nearly got her killed."

Josh looked at her. There it was again, *her killed*, why was everyone suddenly considering the ship as a living thing? “Look Mira. I don’t like being lost like this. What happened today nearly got us all killed. The Captain trusts me to get us home, but I need someone I can trust on the bridge working weapons.”

Before Mira could respond the *Raven* jolted sideways and the ship let out a groan of protest. Josh looked at Mira. Neither needed to say anything. They took off running towards the bridge.

They just passed the crews quarters when an alarm sounded, and an announcement boomed all across the ship, “All hands to your stations. This is an alpha code situation.” That meant the *Raven* was in immediate danger of being destroyed. It was the one call Josh had hoped never to hear. He and Mira basically skidded around the corner to the elevator. All around them crew rushed to their stations. The elevator was packed, but Josh and Mira squeezed on.

Josh’s communicator beeped, “Helm Master to Bridge immediately.”

This is bad, Josh thought to himself. If the Captain was that impatient then the ship was facing a serious threat. The doors to the elevator slid open to a barrage of red flashing lights.

“Helm Master to your position now!” the Captain yelled. Josh quickly took his seat, Mira beside him, and assessed the situation. Somehow the *Raven’s* hull integrity had dropped 60%.

"What happened sir?" Josh asked. There was no response. The Captain was busy up calling orders to others.

"Sir, Vessel approaching, Hunter classification," Mira reported. The bridge fell silent except for the alarms. A hunter class was a bad thing. It meant the ship had the fire power to destroy the *Raven* a couple of times over, but what was it doing in the *Time Stream?*

"Helm Master get us out of here," the Captain ordered. Josh complied and slid the *Raven* into the wall of the *Time Stream.* The ship shuddered but didn't exit. The Stream threw the *Raven* back and into the other wall. The hull integrity dropped another two percent.

Josh tried again, but with the same results. "I can't exit!" There was a response from the Captain but it was drowned out by the sound of an explosion. More alarms blared.

"Warning hull breach. Sealing Rear Compartments thirty-six to forty" the computer called. Josh's heart sank. A hull breach inside the Time Stream could very well be the end of the *Raven* and her crew. He jammed his yaw controls hard and spun the *Raven* around. They hit the walls, the ship shuddered and the image of a horrifying aggressor filled the windshield. They caught only a glimpse of its sleek design and large cannons before a purple flash enveloped the *Raven.* They got out, but barely.

On board the *Mocking Bird*, Bridge

Date: Unknown

Time: Unknown

Location: Time Stream

Captain Tanner nervously drummed his fingers on his arm rest. He was watching as his ship's predecessor, the *Raven*, struggle as it approached. The ship tried to exit the Time Steam without success. The Stream was too violent to exit here, the *Raven* was trapped.

"We have a firing solution sir," the *Mocking Bird's* First Officer stated. The *Mocking Bird* was modeled after the *Raven,* with the flaws removed. With input from the Masters on board the *Raven,* the designers had made an improved navigation system, firing system, flight control system and so on, allowing the ship to navigate the Time Stream with ease. That was why it was the vessel selected to hunt down and destroy the *Raven*.

Tanner didn't like his orders, but he was going to follow them to the letter.

"Fire." An explosion ripped open the side of the *Raven*. It would only be a matter of time now.

"Reloaded and ready to fire," the First Officer reported. The one flaw in the *Mocking Bird* was that the weapons had to be re-aimed and reloaded for every shot. It was time where the vessel was vulnerable to attack. Luckily no one on the *Raven* would know that.

"Target is turning," the Weapons Master shouted.

Tanner looked to the front and sure enough the *Raven* had spun around to face them, "Sound collision alarm. Evasive maneuvers." A high-pitched beep sounded three times in quick succession. Then the *Raven* fired and disappeared. The *Mocking Bird* slammed into the wall of the Time Stream. The ship shuddered and groaned while alarms blared.

"Position report?" Tanner asked.

"They exited sir."

"Follow them!"

The Helm Master looked at the Captain, "There is no way we will make it sir. It's a miracle they did."

Tanner slammed his fist on his arm rest. This was the thing he was worried about. The *Raven*, although less advanced and weaker than the *Mocking Bird*, had a combination that made it a formidable opponent. The Helm Master and Weapons Master were a hard team to beat.

Tanner looked to the First Officer, "I want to know where they ended up and I want you to find them now!"

"That hit knocked out the weapons system sir."

"Unbelievable."

On board the *Raven*; Bridge

Date: August 4, 1985

Time: 13h00 zulu

Location: Montmagny, Québec, Canada

Josh guided the crippled *Raven* over the Canadian landscape. Their exit had been costly, worsening the damage to their hull and nearly ripping the already damaged number four engine off its supports. The area they had ended up in wasn't ideal for hiding the *Raven*. There were mountains on the American side of the large St. Lawrence River but the Captain had ordered them down the middle of the river. The *Raven*'s color would help hide it from onlookers on either of the shores as they were so far apart but Josh didn't like being so exposed.

Josh looked at his navigation display, "There are islands up ahead."

There was a long pause as the Captain came over. He pointed to a small little island at the end of the cluster, "There. Batteur-Des-Loups-Marines. It's small and hard to access. There is a small hunting camp on it. I doubt anyone will be there this time of year." Josh gave the Captain an enquiring look. "It's a long story."

Josh brought the ship in. The island was bigger than he had thought. There was a large, high grassed area surrounded lower-lying rocks, mud and a couple of smaller grassed areas.

Josh was just about to set the ship down when the Captain intervened, "Not there. Put it on the grass."

"With all due respect sir. We will only sink into the grass."

"This is low tide here. If we set down on the rocks the ship will be surrounded by water and rocked by current. The grass stays above water all year round," the Captain explained, "That's an order." Josh doubted the tide would make that much of a difference but he followed the order and gently set the *Raven* down on the grass.

He shut down the engines. Then the Captain motioned to him and Mira. "A moment with the two of you?"

Josh gave a nervous glance to Mira, who returned it. "Certainly sir." They made their way to the Captain's cabin before anyone spoke again.

The Captain folded his arms, "What happened back there?"

Josh shook his head, "I don't know sir. The Stream was too violent to exit. I couldn't get us out."

The Captain smiled, "But you did."

Josh nodded, "Yes I did, but it caused significant damage to an already compromised hull."

The Captain looked to Mira, "Weapons Master. What do we know about that ship?"

Mira nodded, “That ship was an attack vessel. It was made for killing, but I don’t think that it was its original propose. The guns seemed almost strapped on. I took a shot at her and suddenly the threat level dropped. Like I had disabled the ship’s weapons or something.”

The Captain’s arms dropped as Josh looked to Mira in surprise, “You fired without my order?”

“Sir, I felt it would be in the best—,” Mira responded.

“That will be all Weapons Master,” the Captain said, running a hand through his short cut hair. Mira left and the Captain turned back to Josh, “If she's right, then that ship has a mission and I don't believe it was a coincidence that we got hit.”

Josh nodded, “It's after us.”

On board the *Raven*; Cargo Bay One

Date: August 15, 1985

Time: 1h00 zulu

Location: Batteur-des-loups-marines Québec, Canada

"Hold her steady!" Doug ordered, as a crate was moved into the newly-repaired cargo bay. The hull breach in the cargo hold had been minor, just a gash in the bay door. Simple, easy to fix and minimal cargo damage. The problem was that the bay was a mess. The breach had caused objects to shift and things had to be moved for the repair crews. Doug was only now getting things back to normal.

He grabbed his manifest, "That's good, set her down. Now get the rest of the bay back in order." Doug made his way to his cabin, running over the manifest as he went. They had everything, but for some reason he couldn't help think something was wrong. That something became apparent when he walked into his quarters. There sitting at his desk was Rook.

Doug let his tablet fall, "Rook?"

Rook looked his way, "Hello Doug."

"You're supposed to be in containment."

Rook gave Doug a smirk, "You can't contain me. Your crew and your host are going to discover that rather quickly."

Doug reached for his communicator, “Let’s get you to sick bay. There’s obviously something wrong. We’ll get it sorted out and everything will be fine.” Doug never heard the shot but he felt the bullet pass through his hand, shattering his communicator.

“That won’t be needed. I just need a new face,” Rook stated grabbing Doug by the neck, “Yes you’ll do nicely.” Doug felt Rook punch him in the gut, except he never withdrew his hand, he pushed further. His hand entered Doug’s abdomen before it started to...melt? Doug felt no pain, only cold icy fingers creeping their way up and around his internal organs. The substance extending from Rook’s arm then wrapped itself around Doug’s spine, working its way up through his spinal cord to his brain. Doug tried to call for help, to breathe, to fight back, but was unable. His body was no longer under his control. The icy fingers wrapped themselves around his brain and everything went black.

On board the *Raven*; Helm Master Cabin

Date: August 15, 1985

Time: 5h00 zulu

Location: Batteur-des-loups-marines Québec, Canada

Josh opened his eyes to his favorite sight. Mira was sleeping peacefully beside him, the two lovers facing each other. Her face, hardened by years of military service, seemed softer even with the military short haircut she always wore, because she refused to learn how to tie a bun. The two of them had fallen asleep last night looking over the camera data from the attack, trying to figure out the best way to fight their adversary. There wasn't much to go on and most of their solutions were incomplete and relied heavily on estimates about the enemy's size, performance, and fire power. They were operating on the assumption that the ship had better defense and weapons then the *Raven*. One tactic was to target the guns mounted on her exterior, only the ship would surely be protected against such an attack.

Josh rubbed his eyes, they had been going over these sorts of problems for so long his brain was hurting as a result. He rolled over only to shoot straight up.

There, sitting in Josh's desk chair, arms folded, was the Captain, “Good Morning Helm Master. I'm not interrupting anything, am I?”

"Captain?" Josh asked stupidly. Naturally, he and Mira were going to get caught when they weren't actually technically doing anything wrong.

"I came to see if you've made any progress. I can see though that may not have been at the forefront of your evening."

"I..I.." Josh stammered.

Mira rolled over, "What's got you up so early Josh?"

The Captain didn't move, "Good morning Weapons Master."

Mira startled and banged her head on the ceiling of Josh's bunk, "Captain?"

"Please tell me you made something of last night that will benefit the ship."

Josh scrambled for his tablet, "Yes we did. We confirmed that the ship after us was in fact, not originally designed as a killer."

"It looks like it bears the same weapons as the *Raven* plus additional 'big guns' on her bow designed to blast open hulls. Those cannons look as if they were added after the vessel's main construction meaning where they attach to the hull would be weaker." Mira continued.

"If we could hit them there, it would limit their ability to fight and give us a chance to get away," Josh explained. "The problem, is the shields they most certainly have covering that area. They would limit our chances to hit them."

"If they are using cannons, wouldn't that mean they would have to drop their shields to attack?" the Captain asked.

Mira nodded, "Yes they would, but I don't think they will use shields."

Josh looked at her, "Why not?"

"If we added cannons to the *Raven* her shields would cut the ends off them. The shields are extremely complicated and can't just be made bigger. Plus, as the Captain stated, we would have to drop shields every time we attacked. This ship is a quick killer. It is meant to come in, destroy and leave without getting shot at. That's where we have them. The *Raven* is maneuverable and has shields we can use. If it comes after us we might be able to outfight that ship." Mira concluded.

"The cannons would also reduce its maneuverability in normal flight, giving us an advantage." Josh stated, getting excited. They might have a chance.

The Captain nodded, "Good. Weapons Master, report to your cabin and prepare for your shift."

"Yes sir," Mira replied and left.

The Captain looked back to Josh, "We have rules for a reason."

"Sir, we simply fell asleep while working," Josh tried, it didn't work.

"I'm not referring to last night. There are a number of rumors circulating the ship about you two, Mira sneaking to your cabin late at night, you visiting hers after I dismissed her. Is there anything I should know?"

Josh winced. He didn't like lying to the Captain but the consequences of the truth were not something he was willing to face. "No sir,"

"I trust you Helm Master, that's no secret. Don't betray my trust. If there is something, make sure the military doesn't find out." With that the Captain left, leaving Josh alone. Had he betrayed his trust? Of course, he had; he was breaking the rules on board the Captain's ship on a daily basis and then expecting the same respect and trust from him as everyone who obeyed the rules. He didn't want things with Mira to end, but he also couldn't betray the Captain much longer before things would change for the worse.

He sighed, *Ain't this some shit.*

On board the *Mocking Bird*, Bridge

Date: August 20, 1985

Time: 14h00 zulu

Location: Saint-Lawrence River Québec, Canada

"We found them," the radar operator called.

Finally, Tanner thought to himself, they had been searching for the *Raven* for days without success. Monitoring radio, T.V, satellite communications, anything that might give them a hint as to where their target might be hiding. Unfortunately, the *Raven* had to exit over Canada, one of the easiest places for them to hide in the world.

He straightened himself in his seat, "Arm forward cannons and prepare to fire."

"We have a lock on."

"Fire," Tanner ordered. The *Mocking Bird's* cannons let loose a tremendous bang just as the *Raven* came into sight. Just before the shot hit, the *Raven* spun upwards faster than Tanner's eyes could follow it. The cannon shot hit the island the *Raven* had been sitting on, leaving a huge creator in its wake.

Damn it, he thought to himself, "They've been expecting us."

"Sir, they're diving on us."

"Evasive maneuvers," Tanner ordered. The *Mocking Bird* rolled onto her side as she pulled away from the *Raven.* One thing was for sure, the cannons mounted on the *Mocking Bird's* bow didn't help her handling. The *Raven* came around right on her, a flash of light erupted from its flank. A crushing explosion rumbled through the *Mocking Bird.* The ship lurched, but stayed stable.

"We took a direct hit on the port engine. Hull is holding, but won't take another shot," the First Officer reported. Tanner drummed his figures. His shields were useless because of the cannons, but he had more fire power than the *Raven,* and as long as the *Raven* thought the *Mocking Bird* had shields then Tanner had the upper hand.

"Turn right into them and hit them hard," he ordered. The *Mocking Bird* turned onto a collision course with the *Raven.* The distance closed rapidly.

"Fire."

The cannons fired again. The *Raven* banked away but not in time. The shot hit her hard. Tanner watched in frustration as the *Raven*'s shields absorbed the impact, resulting in only minor damage to the ship's already scrapped and beaten flank. Now came the biggest threat. The *Raven* was still coming and she was too close for the cannons.

"Target on collision course. T minus five seconds till impact."

Tanner stiffened, "Break right and avoid." A flash filled the bridge as the *Raven's* lasers hit the *Mocking Bird's* cannons. The shot obliterated the port side cannon and damaged the two remaining ones. If they took another hit like that they would lose their advantage. But then again maybe they wouldn't. The cannons could be jettisoned and if the *Raven's* shields were weakened by the first shot, then they might be able to crush her rather than blow her up. It was a long shot, but worth a try. They would never see it coming.

"Sir, Weapons report starboard cannons damaged but operable. Port and center cannons now inoperable."

Tanner nodded, "Bring her around and prepare to jettison cannons." Tanner got a questioning look from the First Officer. He didn't want to make his intention seem excessive so he presented a reasonable motivation, "We need shields if we're going to beat her."

The First Officer nodded, "Prepare cannons for jettison."

"Target's running bearing one-niner-four-point-six," the Radar Operator reported.

"Pursue and destroy." The *Mocking Bird* followed the *Raven* and got into a good firing position behind her. From this angle they could take out each of her engines easily.

"Why let us get here?" Tanner asked the First Officer as the Weapons Master aimed the cannons.

Suddenly, the Frist Officer said, "She has rear facing lasers!"

Tanner felt his eyes widen, "Break and run!" It was too late and the flash from the *Raven* destroyed what was left of the *Mocking Bird's* cannons. Then a second flash hit in the belly as she made her turn away. The lights flickered as the ship skidded through the sky.

"Damage report," Tanner demanded.

"Hull breach in cargo holds one, two and three, in addition to the galley and female crew quarters. Engines holding strong but port won't survive another hit. All forward cannons are inoperable. All other weapon systems operational. Controls are slow but responsive. Expected to recover soon," the First Officer reported.

"Activate shields on full power and circle back. The *Raven's* shields must be damaged from our hit. I want them to receive everything we've got left. Understood?"

The First Officer nodded, "Yes sir." A shriek filled the bridge as the Remnants of the *Mocking Bird's* forward cannons ripped free, leaving a huge gash in the ship's bow. "Hull breach in forward compartments."

No shit, Tanner thought, "Find the *Raven* and make her pay."

On board the *Raven*; Bridge

Date: August 20, 1985

Time: 14h10 zulu

Location: Saint-Lawrence River Québec, Canada

Josh pulled the *Raven* around hard. When the enemy ship came for them they were able to get above her, and fire. Unfortunately, she turned and their lasers hit the wrong spot. It was clear, though, that Mira's assumption they wouldn't have shields up when engaging was correct. The fact their shot didn't break through meant that the enemy vessel had a much stronger hull than anticipated. The *Raven* took a bad hit; the shields sustained heavy damage and wouldn't have lasted another encounter if Mira hadn't disabled the other ship's cannons and breached their hull with the last shot.

"Their shields are up now," the Defense Master called, "Our shields still holding at 30%."

"They'll have lasers," Mira commented as she worked on another firing solution, "I don't know if I can break their shields in time."

"You better, Weapons Master. Helm Master, make sure they don't hit us again," the Captain ordered. Josh didn't respond. He was too busy nursing the limping *Raven*. She wasn't in top fighting condition. The hull breach they had repaired earlier still needed to be watched and her rear port engine was giving him trouble. He caught a flash from the corner of his eye as the enemy fired. Josh rolled the *Raven* and the laser shot missed. They also got their first good look at their assailant.

"Mocking Bird," the Captain read aloud. Josh watched as the battered but functional *Mocking Bird* steered straight onto them. It was an impressive ship. The same size as the *Raven* but definitely designed for combat. Mira fired, but their shields absorbed the energy before it could do any damage. The *Raven* may have taken the *Mocking Bird's* cannons away but they were still losing the battle. It was only a matter of time before the *Raven* failed.

Then Josh thought of something. "Captain you trust me?"

"Yes Helm Master. What are you thinking?"

Josh tightened his restraints, "Sound the collision alarm and divert power to the starboard shields." The Captain hesitated slightly then nodded and the alarm sounded. Josh pushed the *Raven* as fast as he could and then at the last second broadsided her to the turning *Mocking Bird*. They hit hard with a dazzling display of colorful sparks and explosions along their shield lines as the two ships rocked and slid out of control.

On board the *Mocking Bird*, Bridge

Date: August 20, 1985

Time: 14h13 zulu

Location: Saint-Lawrence River Québec, Canada

"Target turning onto us...collision in T-minus 5 seconds," the Radar Operator called.

Tanner looked out the windshield. The threat display clearly showed the *Raven* speeding right to them. "Hard to starboard!" The *Mocking Bird*s nose swung around but it wasn't fast enough. The *Raven* hit them broadside, the shields sparking from the impact. The *Mocking Bird* slid off into a backwards dive as the *Raven* skidded into a spiral climb.

"Damage report," Tanner demanded.

"No additional damage but shield integrity has dropped and is holding at 10%," the First Officer reported. Tanner couldn't believe it. The *Raven* was never designed as an offensive aircraft. Its weapons were designed to simply defend it long enough so that it could escape into the safety of the Time Stream, yet here it was flying an effective offensive. He cursed his luck knowing all too well that the only reason the ship could fly this way was that their Helm Master and Weapons Master were better than his.

As the *Mocking Bird* regained control, Tanner thought of something. "Turn head onto the *Raven*. Helm Master, hit them with our shields." There was slight hesitation from the First Officer but he gave the order. If the *Raven*'s hit had damaged the *Mocking Bird's* shields as much as it had, then it surely would have decimated the *Raven's* shields as well, leaving them open to attack.

"Arm forward laser and prepare to fire. Let's give them a taste of their own medicine," Tanner ordered. The distance between the ships closed rapidly as it became apparent that the *Raven* had no fear of playing chicken. The *Raven* was burned black on one side from the collision and didn't look at all like she was capable of fighting much longer. What bothered Tanner was that they kept pushing. They had a goal and it wasn't completed yet. Whatever that goal was it couldn't be good for the *Mocking Bird*.

He readjusted his display, "Hold steady. Sound collision alarm."

"*Raven* is firing!" The *Mocking Bird's* Weapons Master called. Sure enough, flashes of light erupted from the oncoming ship.

"Shield integrity decreasing...shields have failed! I repeat shields have failed!" the Defense Master reported.

Damn it, Tanner thought. "Fire everything we've got." The *Raven* pulled herself into a knife edge turn, making herself perpendicular to the ground as the *Mocking Bird's* lasers fired. As the two ships passed each other they raked their opponent's hull. The *Raven* got more hits on the

Mocking Bird as it seemed her weapons were faster than his own. The *Mocking Bird* shook and the lights flashed. Another hit sent sparks flying from overhead, igniting a small fire in the bridge. Red lights flashed and multiple alarms sounded.

"Full integrity report," Tanner yelled.

"Multiple hull breaches on lower hull, forward upper hull, and port hull. Port engine is severely damaged. Shield generator has been destroyed. It is unlikely it can be repaired. Forward cannons are disabled, power is out to most of the ship and the weapons system is disabled."

Tanner shook his head; *The Raven knew where to hit us*. "Report on the *Raven*?"

"Turning onto heading two-niner-niner, one o'clock position," the Radar Operator reported. Tanner looked out and saw their target. It wasn't flying normally, but not for her damage. The *Raven's* engines had tilted into their Time Stream configuration. They had completed their objective. They had rendered the *Mocking Bird* almost useless in combat and were now getting out.

Tanner smiled to himself and rubbed his forehead. *That's one hell of a crew.*

On board the *Raven*; Bridge

Date: Unknown

Time: Unknown

Location: Time Stream

Josh stabilized the *Raven* inside the Time Stream and let himself breathe. They had done it. The Captain began to clap and the whole bridge joined in. Josh looked to Mira who smiled. The *Mocking Bird* was now much less of a threat. They had ripped the cannons clear off their enemy's frame and had decimated their defense systems. It hadn't been without cost. The *Raven* was badly beaten. Although her hull held strong, power was out to everything but the vital systems. Her rear starboard engine had sustained even more damage and she was burned. Even part of the windscreen was blackened from Josh's stunt with the shields. Thankfully the *Raven's* shields had protected her from the worst of it, and they would again, once they recharged. Josh felt a hand shake his shoulder.

"You two are one hell of a team," the First Officer said enthusiastically.

Josh looked to the Captain who was laughing. "Brilliant job, Helm Master."

"Good thinking with the shields. No one would have ever thought of that," The Defenses Master praised.

Josh looked to Mira. Whatever hesitation she had had before about firing on another ship, it was gone now, “You did good.”

Mira smiled, “Thanks. I needed to hear that.”

“Is the ship stable without you Helm Master?” the Captain asked.

“I’m not sure sir. If it’s all right with you I would like to stay with her a little longer till we find out how the damage affects her,” Josh responded.

The Captain nodded, “Good man.”

On board the *Raven*; Captains quarters

Date: Unknown

Time: Unknown

Location: Time Stream

Captain Anderson sat heavily on his bunk. The Helm Master and Weapons Master had done well, there was no doubt about that, but it didn't change the truth. They had broken the rules and he couldn't help feeling betrayed. Anderson knew there would be consequences for the both of them if the military found out, and for him if he let them continue to serve. There was also one further undisputable fact though. The *Raven* would never make it home without them. Anderson grabbed the box sitting at the foot of his bed. He had found the item shortly after their departures. Inside was a simple note that said,

The Helm Master is the Raven's true Master. He will save the lives of everyone onboard.

Sincerely,

Your Mentor

The note was written in the hand-writing of the man the Captain trusted most, the one who had helped him, both personally and professionally, to where he was now. The only problem was that the man was also dead. He had been the Captain of the *Raven*'s predecessor. Not many knew the full details of what had happened onboard that ship. Named *Black Bird*, the *Black Bird* had successfully entered the Time Stream but the medical effects of the Stream on the crew had not then been known. *Black Bird* was almost a ghost ship by the time she had made it back. As far as Anderson knew, the ship had gone into the Time Stream and was quickly pushed back out, but this note suggested that the ship went into the future and back, it made it back home. Only a fraction of the crew had survived. Had his mentor really risked his own life and those of his crew to put a small box on the *Raven?* And what was the significance to the note that exceeded the goal of getting the *Raven* and her crew back home alive?

Anderson forced the thoughts from his mind and opened the camera data from the *Raven*. He wanted to verify what he had seen when they made their final pass by the *Mocking Bird*. He only had half of the usual coverage as the *Raven*'s starboard cameras were damaged when the Helm Master took out the *Mocking Bird's* shields. It was sufficient to confirm his suspicion. On the *Mocking Bird's* beaten flank there was the symbol of *their* military proudly displayed.

Why would our own people hunt us down? he asked himself.

A knock came at the door, "Captain? You asked to see me?"

Anderson straightened his uniform, "Enter Helm Master." Josh walked in and sat in his usual spot, "I wanted your take on something."

"Certainly," Josh stated eagerly.

"The *Mocking Bird* is one of ours," Anderson stated bluntly. He saw no reason to soften anything. If the past was any indication, the Helm Master thought well with cold hard facts.

Josh frowned, "I suspected by the way they knew how to hit us. Why hunt your own people?"

"That's my conundrum. I don't know why they would. What threat could we pose?"

Josh looked at the display showing the pictures of the *Mocking Bird*, "What if...No that wouldn't be it."

"What if what, Helm Master?"

"What about Rook? We know he's not Rook, but he's something we don't understand. What if he's the real reason that they were after us?" Josh proposed.

"Why would you think that?"

"The security officer who froze him mentioned that the creature had said things like 'I'm going to take your host'. What if it's a parasite? If it was living in the ship we plowed into, the same one the real Rook and his team were sent to, then maybe he's more dangerous than we first thought." Josh explained.

Anderson leaned back in his seat, "So what does it want from us? It's clearly too big to take a human as a host and the *Raven* is a machine." Anderson watched as the gears turned inside his Helm Master's head.

"That's assuming it needs something biological to take as a host," Josh said eventually, "We don't know where we were when we hit that thing, but we do know the Time Stream leads to other dimensions. Maybe this thing is a living machine."

"If it's a machine, then it needs power to run," Anderson observed.

"What better power source than the four huge plasma core engines that the *Raven* has," Josh suggested.

Anderson rubbed his forehead as a thought came to him, "What if this thing acts like a virus?"

"I don't understand your meaning, Captain," Josh stated.

"It wants to 'take our host' as you said. Not feed off it, take it. What if it plans to assume control of the *Raven?*'

Anderson watched as Josh's face grew dark, "If this thing made it back to earth, it could multiply and assume control of any machine on the planet."

Anderson tilted his head, "I suppose in theory yes."

“Considering how aggressive this creature is, what do you think would be able to stop a fleet of unmanned power-hungry machines lead by the *Raven* under the control of this thing?” Josh asked.

“Considering our military is almost all unmanned vehicles now, there would be nothing to stop this thing,” Anderson replied grimly.

“It must be why the *Mocking Bird* is after us. They’ve come to stop us from bring this creature back to earth.”

The Captain grabbed his communicator, “Security Command, what is the status on Rook?”

“We’ll check him right now for you, Captain.” There was a pause before the results of the check came, “He’s...uhm...gone, sir.”

Anderson killed the call, “Rook’s gone.”

“If I’m right—”

“We are in big trouble.”

On board the *Raven*; Bridge

Date: Unknown

Time: Unknown

Location: Time Stream

The Captain wasted no time as he and Josh entered the bridge, "Lock down the *Raven*. I want guards posted at all vital compartments and search teams covering every inch of the ship."

"Josh, what happened?" Mira asked.

"Helm Master, how long do we have on the blood filters?" the Captain asked before Josh could answer Mira.

"Three or four days max," Josh replied, "if we're lucky."

The Captain nodded "Keep us in as long as possible."

Josh leaned over to Mira, "Rook escaped."

The Captain moved to the front of the bridge, "Defense Master, I want a direct feed into Security Command."

"Right away sir."

"Weapons Master, do you have anything to help defend the *Raven* internally?"

"No sir. All weapons are exterior." Mira answered quickly. Josh had never seen the Captain like this. He seemed unsettled, but calm and organized at the same time.

"Security Command feed is active," the Defense Master reported.

Mira quickly checked her display, "What about Alt sir. He beat this thing once. His input might help now."

The Captain shot a look at Josh, "Get Alt here immediately."

On board the *Raven*; Bridge

Date: Unknown

Time: Unknown

Location: Time Stream

"No luck yet sir. The creature's still missing," the First Officer reported.

"I want a report from each station. See if anyone else is missing," the Captain ordered.

Josh jumped when he felt something bump his seat, "So this is where you control her, is it?"

Josh nodded to Alt, "Her flight controls anyway." Alt didn't look good. He was in a wheel chair, heavily bandaged from head to toe and was sort of slumping to one side as his back wasn't strong enough to support his weight yet.

"Amazing," Alt commented, "I heard about the *Mocking Bird.* That was some pretty impressive flying."

Josh shuddered a little. Although no one had said anything to him, it was a stupid move to use the *Raven's* shields as a weapon. If it hadn't worked, or the *Mocking Bird* had had secondary shields, he would have doomed them all. The only reason the crew was praising him instead of hating him was that he got lucky.

"Enjoying your visit?" the Doctor asked.

"Very much so," Alt responded.

Josh smiled, "I thought you were going to be helping us?"

"I am. How much can you move this thing inside the Time Stream?"

Josh shrugged again, "Not much. I can roll, maybe make a turn or two, but nothing more. We risk hitting the wall if I do much more."

"You weren't concerned with hitting things when it came to the *Mocking Bird*," the Doctor observed.

"Helm Master? Doctor? A moment please?" the Captain requested. Josh complied and got to the Captain's side as quickly as possible. "No one can find Load Master Doug anywhere."

"The creature might have already found him," Josh stated.

The Captain nodded, "My concern runs deeper than that. This thing mimicked Rook. What's stopping him from doing it again once its original disguise failed?"

"It would be possible," the Doctor added, "I've been thinking about what you two said about this creature. It's clearly not human. It's obviously an alien creature of some kind. I'd speculate that like creatures on earth it won't generally take unsteady action. It would want to conserve energy till it can find another food source. If its intention is to take control of the *Raven* and feed off its engines then maybe its attack against the crew is acting on instinct trying to defend itself long enough to get the food it needs to survive."

Josh raised an eyebrow, "Hitting us where he could blow us up is for survival?"

The Doctor shook his head, "I don't think it thinks the *Raven* is a machine. From talking with Alt, it seems to think it's a living creature. So, it's probably confused."

"Alt also said we killed it. I thought it referred to the ship we hit on our first exit," Josh stated.

"What if it uses ships as a host," Mira interjected. All four men turned to look at her.

The Doctor smiled, "Brilliant. It is simply looking for a host! You have one great team here Captain."

"I'm well aware. So how do we beat it? Unless it attacks the engines again we can't very well freeze it." the Captain observed.

"Send the Helm Master," Mira suggested.

Josh sent her a death glare, "My place is here at the Helm."

"Elaborate, Weapons Master, please," the Captain prompted.

"The Helm Master treats this ship like his baby. Maybe, if this thing is like a ship, the Helm Master could take it," Mira explained.

"I think you're over estimating the similarities between this creature and a machine. I mean when it went after me with..." Alt drifted off, "It had rage in its eyes. It seemed emotionless but at the same it couldn't be emotionless if it was angry...no there's no way it could be bonded with."

The Captain drummed his fingers, "I agree with Alt. It's too risky. Helm Master, that will be all."

***

It had been hours since Mira's suggestion to send Josh after Rook. Although he hated the idea he couldn't get it out of his head. He ran his hands over his controls. He smiled a little, imagining if the *Raven* were alive, how they could work as a team. Man and machine working in harmony. He quickly pulled himself out of his train of thought. It was bad to think that way. He needed to have no hesitation should it come to the Captain's back-up plan.

A pistol tapped his shoulder, "You might want this."

Josh accepted the pistol from Alt, "How do you do it?"

"Easy, point and shoot."

Josh laughed nervously, "I mean kill."

"The same way you killed the *Mocking Bird*, it's a threat, you eliminate it." Alt explained. He now understood Mira's original hesitation at firing the *Raven's* weapons.

Josh thought of something. "Sir. If this thing disables the control system, I'll have to exit, or we risk getting ripped apart."

The Captain frowned, "You're right Helm Master. Keep her in as long as possible."

***

They flew on for a good hour without results. Josh could tell that Alt was getting worried. He himself was getting worried. *Where was Rook*? It's not like he could just disappear. As if to answer his question, the bridge door slid open and there it was, standing looking at the crew, one arm ending in a mass of rusted metal. No one moved. No one even dared to breathe, afraid of what was coming.

"Out," the creature, now disguised as the Load Master, Doug, commanded. Still, no one moved. Instantly the creature was by the Defense Master's side, and the man fell to the floor, his leg twisted at an unnatural angle. That's when the first shot flew. A torrent of machine gun fire ripped into the creature. The creature fell but got back up, wounds clearly visible. It scanned the whole bridge and locked eyes with Josh. It moved towards him, but the Captain stepped between them. The creature never hesitated. It grabbed the Captain by the neck and lifted him off his feet.

"All of you out! Or it dies," the creature shouted. Whether it knew the significance of the man it was holding was lost to Josh, but one thing was for sure. They needed that man alive. The Captain nodded his head; slowly and cautiously everyone cleared out but Mira and Josh.

Mira stepped towards the monster hijacker, "We aren't leaving until you let him go."

The creature smiled, "You leave now and I throw it after you. Now move it."

"No," Mira stated sternly.

"Mira. Go," Josh insisted.

"I am not–" Mira stopped when she looked at Josh. He had a plan and she would only get in the way, or worse, get hurt.

Her arms dropped and she bowed her head, "I'm sorry Captain."

"You too." The creature ordered.

Josh drew his weapon, "Drop him."

"Excuse me?"

"I said drop him," Josh commanded. The creature laughed. Josh didn't hesitate, he fired. It was an amazing shot. It ripped through the creature's arm and the Captain fell to the floor gasping for air. The creature looked to Josh. Its eyes cold as ice. It raised what was left of its arm. It looked like it was trying to reform the rest but it was unsuccessful.

"Not a bad shot," It grimaced and grabbed the Captain's gun. The hole in its arm had not repaired but it didn't seem to affect the thing's ability to fire a gun. Josh ducked for cover as a shot ripped into an electrical panel causing a shower of sparks. Alarms blared as some of the bridge equipment lost power. He hadn't thought this through. He had been lucky up to this point but felt like that luck was about to run out. He had hoped this thing would just give up. Looking at it now though, it was apparent how naïve he had been. He could hear a scuffle and when he turned around, he saw the creature holding the Captain in front of him, gun aimed and ready to shoot. It fired but no bullets flew. There was a simple click as the gun dry fired.

"What kind of idiot loads one bullet?" The creature asked, shuffling to use the Captain as a more effective shield. The creature must have had some mortal vulnerability if it was protecting itself in this way, but Josh couldn't figure out why.

"Let him go," Josh yelled. He had no idea where this confidence was coming from. He normally would have followed Mira, leaving the Captain to his own devices. But no, he felt a sense of pride standing up for his ship, "And leave my ship."

The creature laughed, "Leave? But the fun is just beginning. Now, why don't you run off and leave me and, Captain, you called it— to ourselves."

"I'm not warning you again," Josh stated firmly and raised his weapon.

"You won't shoot. You got lucky last time. If you shoot now, you'll shoot your beloved Captain."

Josh looked at the Captain, who nodded, "Shoot me Helm Master." Josh was caught off guard, "That's an order Helm Master!"

"Sir—"

"If you don't, you will leave me no choice but to pull you from your position disobeying a direct order!" the Captain persisted.

Josh's hand began to shake as he took aim. He steadied himself, placing his non-shooting arm under his shooting arm. He then took aim at the creature's head, "Then relieve me," he said as he pulled the trigger. The shot hit the monster square in the face, blowing a large hole where its left eye had been. It staggered backwards. Josh took advantage of the exposed target. He emptied his magazine into the creature, adding to a collage of wounds already inflicted. He then rushed to the Captain's side. Without saying a word, he grabbed the man's tactical knife.

"Stand down!" the Captain called but Josh didn't listen. He knew one thing. The *Raven* was at risk as long as this thing lived. He cornered it, pushing it up against the wall, the knife to its neck.

"What do you want?" Josh demanded.

The creature smiled, "A home. You took mine after all."

Josh pushed the blade deeper causing a shallow cut, not that the creature seemed to mind, "Well, you can't have mine."

The creature scoffed, "How about I kill you? Will that make things easier?" With that the creature grabbed Josh's blade and drove it into Josh's abdomen. Josh felt the metal pierce his skin. The creature left the blade in Josh as he staggered backwards, clutching his wound.

How was I so stupid? The Captain warned me but I didn't listen, Josh thought. He looked to the Captain.

"Helm Master!" the man called. He saw the disappointment and fear behind the normally neutral eyes. Man, had Josh ever blown it. He had one last hope. He staggered to the helm and typed a command into the computer, leaving bloody finger marks as he did so.

"If you move," he muttered to the creature, "I blow us all up." Josh saw a shift in the creature, it seemed nervous.

"Helm Master!" the Captain called again, more forcefully.

"You may have killed me but I can still take the *Raven* with me."

"You would not. You are unable to die for your host. That has become apparent in my observation of your species," the creature insisted, the urgency behind his voice betraying his neutral demeanor.

"The rest of the crew might not, but I am." Josh said firmly and hit the execute button.

"Warning. Ship Self-Destruct Sequences activated. T minus ten minutes till detonation. Exit Time Stream and prepare all evacuation pods for deployment," the computer cautioned.

"Turn it off!" The creature screamed. It lunged for Josh. That's when Josh did the only thing he could do. He pushed the *Raven* out of the Time Stream. It threw it into a spin knocking the Creature and Josh to the floor. Josh grabbed the blade in his abdomen and with a cry of pain pulled it from his wound. Blood gushed out from the hole it left. He stood up and lunged at the creature. He got its head between his knees and slashed. The monster's head fell clean off, landing as a pile of slime on the floor. Soon the whole creature melted, leaving nothing but a pool of sticky reddish slime mixed with Josh's own blood. The Captain stayed silent, stunned. Josh crawled to the helm controls, quickly aborted the count down and leveled the ship.

"Self-Destruct Sequence aborted," were the last words he heard before blacking out.

On board the *Raven*; Sick Bay

Date: Unknown

Time: Unknown

Location: Time Stream

Josh woke up to burning bright white lights. He groaned, feeling the pain of his wound. He looked to see Mira at the side of the bed. She had a furious expression on her face.

"You are a true idiot," she accused. Josh nodded. He agreed. He didn't think it was possible to screw up more than he had.

"Thank you for leaving," he said weakly.

"Next time I'm staying."

The door slid open, "Ah Helm Master. Good to see you awake," the Doctor said. He was followed by Alt and the Captain.

"Man, Helm Master. I gave you the gun but never figured you would use it," Alt said with a chuckle.

"You alright Captain?" Josh asked.

"You disobeyed a direct order," he stated.

"I shot, I just missed," Josh responded.

Alt released a strong laugh, "One hell of a miss."

Josh looked to the Doctor, “How bad did it get me?”

The Doctor sighed heavily, “It really ‘got you’ as you say. The knife did extensive damage to your stomach and liver. We patched most of the damage. It looks like the creature was aiming for your lungs, but somehow missed. You lost a lot of blood by pulling that knife. You’ll be living on nothing but fluids for the next while. You’ll live, but barely. You were...” the Doctor trailed off as if trying to find the right adjective.

“Thick skulled,” Mira suggested.

“Brave,” Alt countered.

“Loyal,” the Captain stated.

The Doctor smiled, “I was thinking lucky, but any of those would suffice.”

The Captain sat in a chair, “Helm Master, you asked that thing what it wanted; what did it say?”

Josh had to think for a moment before responding, “It wanted a home.”

Alt’s eyes shifted, “It is looking for a host.”

“I’ve been thinking about this,” Mira stated, “Maybe the Doctor’s right. About it thinking the *Raven* is alive. If what we saw in that dimension were living machines, then when a creature like this thing went after one, it would need to beat its immune system. Maybe that's what it thought we are."

Josh sat up, forcing through the pain in his side, "It went after the bridge thinking it was the brain."

"It would explain its behavior. But why try to kill the ship and why engage with the Helm Master and Captain?" the Doctor asked.

"It didn't want to kill the *Raven*. If it needs the ship to survive, then the relationship would have to be symbiotic so the host had to survive. I don't, however, know about the attack on the Helm Master and the Captain."

"Because we were the ones it considered a threat. Everyone followed our orders. If it took us out it must have thought the whole system would fall apart."

Alt looked to the Captain, "The Helm Master doesn't give orders. Does he?"

Everyone's eyes went to the floor. "The Helm Master disobeyed my order and ordered the Weapons Master off the bridge. The confusion would be easy enough," the Captain explained.

Josh shifted himself so his leg was off the side of the bed, then he thought of something, "Where is it now?"

"We don't know," Mira said bluntly.

"I turned him into a pile of mush," Josh argued.

The Captain nodded, "Would you please give us the room?" Everyone complied and left.

"I did kill it, didn't I?"

"I need to know one thing. You said that you would never abandon *your* ship. Do you still stand by that statement? Even after risking the lives of every person on board with your self-destruct stunt?" the Captain asked.

The way he said *your ship* made Josh cringe. "I meant it. I'm going to get the *Raven* back home safe, just like you asked."

"The creature disappeared shortly after you lost consciousness."

On board the *Raven*; Bridge Elevator

Date: Unknown

Time: Unknown

Location: Time Stream

Anderson adjusted his blood filter. Though he knew its importance, he found the device irritating to say the least. He stopped playing with the infernal thing as the doors to the elevator slid open. He walked into the bridge to relieve the First Officer.

"What's the status on the computer repairs?" he asked, after he had settled in his seat. The maintenance crew had been in the process of working on a few minor problems with the computer system that had been a result of their engagement with the *Mocking Bird.*

The First Officer fiddled with his console, "Last report was repairs completed, minor door malfunction. They are working on fixing that now."

Anderson nodded, "Excellent." He looked around the bridge. All the main crew were there, but for one. The Helm Master was still recovering. Anderson glanced at the relief helmsman, then to his blood filter. Their batteries wouldn't last another day, but he disliked the idea of forcing the Helm Master to fly the *Raven* before he was ready. At the same time, he didn't trust anyone else to handle the ship during an exit. He looked back to the helm controls. He frowned at the sight of the blood stains on its surface. He hadn't known what had possessed the Helm Master to risk blowing up the ship, but whatever they were, the gamble had paid off, sort of. There was no sign of the creature and a conversation with the Doctor had brought to light the idea that the monster could have simply dissolved. Anderson's thoughts were interrupted by an alarm. The display on the windshield shifted to show a general alarm had been activated in the main computer compartment.

Anderson looked to the First Officer. "I thought the repairs went well?"

"That was the report sir," the First Officer responded.

"Bring up the surveillance camera, will you?" The feed came up moments later. What he saw made his gut wrench. From the camera's vantage point he could clearly see a terrified technician cornered with a red dot on his forehead. He looked to the other side of the image to see a gun extended from the ceiling aimed at the man.

How? He wondered, "Weapons Master, what is the meaning of this?"

"It's not me sir—"

"You informed me of no internal defenses. Yet we seem to have them."

The Weapons Master turned to her display, "We shouldn't sir. I'll—I'm locked out of my console."

The Captain came up behind her, sure enough her console had locked, "What kind of repairs were they making to the computer?" Before he could get a response, the forward display shifted, shoving the camera feed to the left, and displayed the words.

Bring the one you call Helm Master to the bridge.

Anderson's mouth dropped. He looked to the Weapons Master who wore an equally puzzled expression. He could only think of one thing, that thing hadn't simply dissolved.

Speak. Where is he? The display asked.

Anderson moved back to his seat, "The Helm Master is incapacitated at the moment."

My files detail that his condition is within your species' operational limits. Bring him here now.

"And if I refuse?" In response to his question the gun in the computer department fired, killing the technician trapped inside.

Do not make me find another target.

"First Officer. Have the Helm Master brought up as quickly and as safely as possible."

On board the *Raven*; Bridge

Date: Unknown

Time: Unknown

Location: Time Stream

Josh was carefully placed on a seat, the pain in his side only getting worse as they moved him to the bridge. He was still confused as to why he needed to be here. The blood filters were still running on sufficient power, so an exit would be unnecessary and the bridge had no warning light flashing. Just concerned looks from the crew, most notably Mira, at his condition.

Josh painfully positioned himself behind the helm controls, “Captain? May I ask what I’m needed for?”

“I wish I could tell you Helm Master. I wouldn’t have you here if it wasn’t important though,” the Captain responded. Then the lights went out. Josh moved as quickly as possible to check that the computers hadn’t failed again but found nothing wrong. He looked to the Captain.

“We’re all locked out of our consoles,” the man stated.

Mira leaned over, “Not all. The Helm Master’s controls have unlocked.”

Josh looked to her, “What did I miss?” Before anyone could answer the forward display lit up with the words.

Everyone but the Helm Master must leave the bridge immediately.

Josh looked in bewilderment at the screen. Even more to his surprise, the Captain complied.

"Captain," he protested.

The Captain gave him a nod, "It has already killed one of my men today. We're going to do what it wants for now. Keep the ship alive, will you?"

Josh nodded, but didn't respond verbally. Once everyone was out of the bridge, the words on the display changed.

Your ship has kept very detailed records of you Helm Master. Or would you prefer Josh?

Josh sat still, stunned. This wasn't right. The ship was asking him questions. The ship was alive? His thoughts turned dark as he realized what this meant. The ship seemed to notice this as it continued.

Do not worry. I mean you no harm.

"No harm? I have a knife wound in my stomach that says differently," Josh found himself saying aloud.

I need the *Raven* I believe you call her I need her power supply to live. My actions are all to ensure my survival.

"What do you want?" Josh asked, his voice cold as ice. If that creature had control of the ship it wouldn't mean anything good.

Your ship has altered my being. I have learned of your mission and its ill-conceived navigation system that caused the unwanted result of you of becoming lost. I find it amusing that your kind thinks it can create something as complex as this ship and believe that it would perform flawlessly.

Josh stared at the screen. It was speaking like a human, sort of. Rational thought patterns, something he had always thought would make the *Raven* the most effective ship in the world. Now, though, faced with the reality of his idea, he was more than a little frightened. This creature could kill them all in a matter of seconds, and if they were unlucky it would have that one human trait that was most common. The one to destroy your enemy.

I can sense that you have often thought of the *Raven* as more than just a ship. You think of her as your responsibility and your home. The ship thought that way too. Its performance data was always best with you at the controls. If your Captain's personal logs are anything to go by, you're the only one that can bring it home in one piece. By extension it means that you are the only hope I have of survival. I wish

to serve you as the *Raven* has. I will be your *Raven* and you my Helm Master, providing that you are up to the challenge. If not I will try on my own, but my calculations show that I have a 10% chance of success if I try to exit the Time Stream alone.

Josh once again sat speechless. How could this thing know so much? He supposed it would have access to the *Raven's* files, which would account for most of it, but what about his bond with the machine? And what about the performance data? Sure, he pushed the *Raven* more than the other helmsmen but this thing had mistaken it for the ship "choosing" to fly better with him flying her. The words disappeared and five words appeared on Josh's console display.

Can I count on you?

Josh contemplated his options; he figured it better to appear to be on the side of this thing, "Yes," he replied, "But you have to take orders from all the Masters, including the Captain."

Certainly. May I pose a question?

Josh nodded, still in shock.

Can we utilize the *Mocking Bird*?

On board the *Mocking Bird*, Bridge

Date: August 24, 1985

Time: 17h00 zulu

Location: Bay of Fundy, Canada

"What's the final damage report?" Tanner asked, rubbing his forehead. After their engagement with the *Raven* they had flown east in hope of finding somewhere secluded to land. They had, and at his insistence, they landed. The problem was that he hadn't listened to the computer's warning of an unstable landing surface. The area looked large, relatively flat with only a slight slant, and safe. Only, when they landed, the *Mocking Bird* sank into the mud till she was almost resting on her already damaged belly. Thankfully it hadn't sunk farther or mud would have flooded the lower compartments before the ship settled. They did however have to shut down their engines for fear of ingesting muck into them and now, even if they could get them going again, it was unlikely the damaged engines could pull the *Mocking Bird* free. They were stuck.

Tanner had looked up the history of where they had landed and, much to his displeasure, it was an area known for the world's largest tides. The *Mocking Bird* was sitting right were the water would come. Tanner had considered the possibility of ordering the evacuation of the ship and leave it to the sea. They were in 1985, so his crew could make proper lives here. But the thought of the fate that would become all the men and women, and their families back home if they gave up, made it an impossible call to make.

The First Officer handed the damage report to the Captain, pulling him from his thoughts, "The forward cannons are gone. Shield generator was destroyed beyond repair. The long range lasers are inoperable, although we have short range lasers still functioning. Long range radar is functioning and the firing system has been repaired, but the short-range radar is down. The port engine is heavily damaged. Crews will attempt to repair it but the Engine Master was quick to call it a write off. The starboard engine is functional and relatively undamaged. It will be ready for flight by the morning. The landing gear are trapped in the mud and inoperable at the moment. We are within operational weight limits but barely—"

"Casualty report?" Tanner interrupted.

"No casualties reported."

Tanner gave the First Officer a look, "Pardon."

"All the *Raven*'s hits were strategic. They damaged the ship, not the crew."

One hell of a crew, Tanner thought to himself again. He found it almost amusing that a crew that good would bring about the end of the world.

"Sir!" the Radar Operator called, "New contact, low, bearing one-eight-seven...it's the *Raven*."

What? Tanner thought. The *Raven* had done its damage. How did it find its way back? And more importantly, why was it back? The answer deeply troubled Tanner.

Tanner sighed, "Arm short range lasers."

"They won't break their shields," the Weapons Master informed him.

"Arm them anyway." Tanner insisted. It was better than nothing. In minutes, the *Raven* was hovering in front of the *Mocking Bird's* bridge. Her four engines were constantly changing their angle to deal with the wind. It was a sight to see, yet another testament to her Helm Master's skill.

Then the *Mocking Bird*s windshield shattered. Tanner instantly threw himself to the floor. When no other gunshots were fired, he looked up to find a spike embedded in the wall. It only took him a second to recognize what it was. It was the instrument used for the reproduction of the monster that the *Raven* would bring back with her. It acted much like an egg, implanting a new creature in the afflicted target. That meant that it had already assumed control of the *Raven*, and now it had the *Mocking Bird*. The spike dissolved and melted into the wall, fusing seamlessly with the metal.

Tanner knew what came next, “Activate the self-destruct sequence and evacuate!” His order was too late as all the screens in the bridge blacked out.

On board the *Raven*; Bridge

Date: August 24, 1985

Time: 17h15 zulu

Location: Bay of Fundy, Canada

The forward display read:

Mocking Bird captured,

Josh shifted uneasily. He didn't like the idea of taking over another's ship, even if it was their best chance of getting home. Their plan was for the creature to capture the *Mocking Bird* and have her guide the *Raven* home. They dropped the *Mocking Bird's* crew back in their own time. A good plan, but looking at the ship now it didn't look promising that the *Mocking Bird* would even fly.

"Report on her status?" the Captain asked.

Functional.

The Captain nodded and grabbed a microphone, "*Mocking Bird* this is Captain Anderson of the *Raven,* do you read? Over."

Josh paid little attention to the Captain's radio communication. It was basically telling the *Mocking Bird's* crew their plan. It was more a courtesy then anything. The *Mocking Bird* crew had no say in the matter.

Josh's main focus was on keeping the *Raven* in her position. Words swirled onto his display.

There is a problem. The *Mocking Bird* landed in mud. Her landing gear are stuck. In addition, I must congratulate the Weapons Master. You did a wonderful job of rendering her useless in combat.

Josh looked to Mira, who looked like she didn't know how to respond, "Can it get out?"

Negative. A VOLT take off is out of the question. Her port engine is too damaged to start. Only option is a normal take off but there is too much mud for her to move.

"Could we lift her out with the *Raven*?" Mira asked.

Josh shook his head, "The *Raven* was never designed for that. Her engines aren't strong enough. Not to mention the frame."

There's more. Where the *Mocking Bird* is sitting will be under water in a matter of hours. The tide is coming in.

"Great," Josh muttered and looked back to the Captain. Maybe tides where a bigger deal then he had originally thought.

"You say that it never assumes control 'till we returned?" he heard Anderson ask the other Captain. The *Raven* wasn't following what was supposed to happen? Had they arrived home earlier in the past? The entire contemplation began to make his head hurt. Why did time travel have to be so confusing? He focused on the problem at hand, freeing the *Mocking Bird*.

"What if she rocked herself?" Mira proposed.

"You mean like when you get a car stuck?" Josh asked.

Mira shrugged, "Sort of. I mean listening to you it's obvious her engines wouldn't respond quickly enough but if she could make a furrow in the mud, long enough, wouldn't she be able to get up speed needed for takeoff."

"She would just slip down the slope." Josh replied. "Can you fix the damaged engine?" he asked

Not before the tide comes in.

Josh let his mind toy with the problem, trying to look at it from the *Mocking Bird's* Helm Master's position. Then he thought of something, it was a long shot, a really long shot, but it could work. "We need her to slide."

Mira gave him a look, "You mean like into the water?"

I share the Weapons Master's doubts.

"If she can gain enough speed going down the slope then her wings might be able to support her." Josh explained.

What about the resistance caused by the landing gear?

Josh grunted. He hadn't thought of that. Josh looked out to the stuck ship. He could almost see it pleading for his help. "Which engine is broken?"

Port side.

"Josh, the *Raven* can take off in a spin, can't she?" Mira asked. Josh nodded. "Why not spin the *Mocking Bird*?"

Josh shook his head then stopped. Why *not* spin the *Mocking Bird*? What about the landing gear though? "Mira. How accurate are the weapons?"

"Depend on who's using them. I'm a pretty good shot if that's what you're asking."

What are you planning Helm Master?

"I second that Helm Master," the Captain said from behind. Josh only realized then how long and loud their debate had been.

"Mi—the Weapons Master suggested we spin the *Mocking Bird* similar to what we did on our offensive against it. The problem is her landing gear. If, once the functioning engine is at full power, the Weapon Master could then shoot off the landing gear. It might set it free."

The Captain raised an eyebrow, "Can you do that Weapons Master?"

"If the Helm Master gets me in the right position." Mira responded.

"Alright do it. I'll notify Captain Tanner of our intentions...*Raven,* notify the *Mocking Bird*,"

***

Mocking Bird is powering up her engine, the creature in control of the *Raven* reported shortly afterward, **Reaching full power**.

Josh maneuvered the *Raven* to give Mira the best angle, "Alright, we're good."

"Fire," the Captain ordered. Three flashes of light erupted from the *Raven* destroying the *Mocking Bird's* landing gear in sequence of nose, starboard rear and finely the port rear. The *Mocking Bird* took off like a shot. Josh threw the *Raven* into a quick reversed flight path to avoid getting hit. The *Mocking Bird's* starboard wing grabbed the mud swinging her around. For a split second, it looked like she was going to roll over, then the wing ripped itself free of the mud and the ship spun up and away. Josh let out a breath he hadn't known he had been holding.

"Well done," he said to Mira.

The *Mocking Bird* can't recover.

Josh looked to see the ship was indeed struggling. He quickly gave the auto pilot control to the *Raven*. "Patch me through to their controls."

"Helm Master. You are not their Helm Master," the Captain stated.

"That maneuver is incredibly difficult to recover from. That thought had escaped me till now. Their Helm Master is unlikely to know what to do," Josh insisted. "Do it or we lose our way home."

You have control, the forward display read.

Josh took the controls of the *Mocking Bird*, ignoring the Captain's protest.

Watching through the *Raven's* windshield, he worked the controls. It was harder than he thought. He had to be careful not to overstress the already-damaged frame, not to mention the fact that he couldn't feel the *Mocking Bird*s movements. He struggled for a few more seconds. The ship didn't appear to be designed to fly on one engine, but he finely got her level. He flew her straight, with the *Raven* following for a few minutes before relinquishing control.

"What is the status of the *Mocking Bird?*" the Captain asked. There was an edge to his voice that worried Josh.

She needs time to heal the engine before entering the Time Stream.

The Captain nodded, "Helm Master. A word please?" Josh complied and followed, ignoring the pain in his side as he limped. They entered the Captain's private cabin without a word spoken. "You are not in command of this ship."

Josh flinched at the Captain's accusing tone, "Sir I–"

"You disobeyed an order to let the *Mocking Bird* fly herself, you disobeyed me in the engagement against Rook. You took the lives of myself and my entire crew into your hands when you slammed the *Raven* into the *Mocking Bird's* shields. You have taken quite a few risks without consulting me. You know I trust you, but that does not mean I think you are above your position." the Captain explained calmly.

Josh nodded, "You're right sir."

"You follow my orders, and so does the ship," the Captain stated firmly. Josh again nodded, but the ship had other plans. A gun materialized from the ceiling and aimed itself at the Captain. Before either man could react, they heard the safety click off and a message displayed on the Captain's personal display panel.

And If I refuse to take orders from you?

Josh gulped. Why was this thing so persistent on not listening to the Captain?

I have been researching your kind. Seems there is always a better man being led by an inferior one. Isn't that right Captain?

Josh looked to the Captain who remained neutral.

You know you are not the Master of the *Raven*.

"Call this off Helm Master."

Josh was about to do just that, but the statement intrigue him, "What is it talking about?"

Go on *Captain*. Tell him. Tell him you've been playing him this whole time.

"The *Raven's* predecessor, *Black Bird,* didn't just bounce back as we suspected," the Captain sighed, "I don't know how long she was flying without NAV in the Time Stream. Her Captain managed to leave one thing on the *Raven* that I know of."

"What did he leave?"

The Captain eyed the gun before continuing, "A box. Inside was a note saying you were the key to our survival. And that you would become the *Raven's* Master."

It is not the Helm Master that must follow orders,

With that a panel, next to Josh slid open, revealing a semi-automatic pistol.

Go and take your position.

Josh looked at the display and the gun. *It doesn't understand loyalty,* he thought to himself. The Captain may have not told Josh the full truth, but he certainly had never lied to him. He took the fire arm and unloaded it, letting it fall to the floor, “I will not shoot my Captain. And neither will you. Disarm your weapon.” Josh commanded. The creature complied.

Yes sir.

On board the *Raven*; Helm Master Cabin

Date: Unknown

Time: Unknown

Location: Unknown

Josh sat heavily on his bunk, pain blooming across his abdomen, he was overdoing it. He ran his hands through his hair, *Great. Just Great.* He thought, *now the Captain will never trust me again.*

You look troubled Helm Master. A message said on Josh's personal display.

"Is there anywhere you can't see me?" he mumbled.

I have access to all cameras onboard.

"There aren't cameras in my cabin."

There is now.

Josh rolled his eyes and fell back on his bunk, completely ignoring the pain. He deserved it anyway. "Why? Why go after the Captain?"

He is a limiting factor to our operations. Your species seems to have the illusion of needing rank where not necessary. You could bring me home alone perfectly fine, instead you are limited by the orders of an inferior commander.

"The Captain is not inferior. He is more than qualified for his position."

You are clearly more fit to command. You have a better relationship with the ship after all.

"Wrong. I have a *correspondence* with you for some reason. Not the ship. The ship is nothing but a shell under the Captain's command. I am not a leader," Josh shot back.

Do you really believe that?

Josh was about to snap but he stopped. Did he believe his own words? He had thought of what it would have been like to fly with the *Raven* instead of just flying her; the way he often anticipated her movements, even the habit of calling the ship a "her". Was it his way of pretending, or wishing she was alive? Thankfully for him a knock on the door interrupted his thoughts.

"Enter," he called. The door slid open revealing Mira.

"Hey. You okay?" she asked, as she entered. Josh didn't respond.

Hello Weapons Master.

"Monster," Mira said coldly.

Please. Address me by *Raven*. It is more fitting.

"You are not the *Raven*," Josh snapped.

Mira placed a hand on Josh's shoulder, "Yelling at it won't solve anything."

Josh sighed, "Alright. *Raven* access your files. Research loyalty and its implications. Chew on that for a while and then get back to me on the validity of my actions." The messages disappeared and the display returned to normal.

"So Mira," Josh began, adjusting himself so he could be more comfortable even with his wounds. It didn't work. "What can I do for you?"

"I heard about the altercation with the Captain. Wanted to make sure you were all right."

Josh shook his head, "Shaken but stable."

Mira smiled, "That's sounds like the man I know."

Josh gave Mira a hug. He recoiled from the embrace as pain shot through his body. He took a deep breath as a thought came to him, "How did you find out?"

"The Captain asked if you were likely to take its advice," Mira replied simply, "I assured him you're as loyal as they come."

Josh grunted, "He is never going to trust me again,"

"It's not like you ordered the ship to do what it did. If what he said is true you ordered it to disarm."

"Yes. But not as per *his* orders. I should have stopped everything as soon as he said to but I wanted to know what he was hiding and pushed, using the *Raven* as my backup," Josh explained.

Mira leaned in to give Josh another hug, but stopped as if remembering that it was not a good idea, "I wouldn't worry about it. I mean if it comes down to it, at least the ship and I trust you."

Josh was about to respond when a message appeared showing that the creature did not understand the researched material in the slightest.

Loyalty will be the downfall of your species.

On board the *Raven*; Bridge

Date: July 24, 3000

Time: 17h15 zulu

Location: Unknown

The sight that greeted the *Raven* and her crew as they recovered from following the *Mocking Bird* out of the Time Stream was shocking. The navigation system told them they were in the right dimension and it was in fact earth, but it was not the earth they knew. They flew over blackened and burning forests. Whole cities lay in ruin all across the landscape. There were no other ships around, no other aircraft, cars, boats, anything. There was no other life. Josh wondered if bringing the *Mocking Bird's* crew home was really what was best for them.

"What happened?" Josh asked, to no one in particularly. The *Raven* answered.

According to the *Mocking Bird*, I did.

Silence returned to the bridge as they flew on. All the while Mira scanned for signs of life, always coming up empty.

"Are we certain we are in the right place?" the Captain asked. Various people, including the ship, confirmed their location, "My God. What did we do?"

I don't understand how I could do all this?

Josh read the message and looked to Mira's display, and still no life detected. "Because you are a monster," Mira grumbled. For some reason, this rubbed Josh the wrong way.

"Was," he corrected, "From what I understand of this timeline, it never assumed control of the *Raven*. Which means it is not the same creature that originally returned with us. Maybe the ship changed it."

Whatever the reason these actions are inexcusable.

Did it just acknowledge responsibility? Was its message regretful? Did it feel sorrow and pain for those it hurt in this timeline? Once again, the complication of time travel made Josh's brain hurt and he forced himself to stop thinking of the subject. Still though, the idea that this thing wasn't truly a monster was planted firmly in Josh's mind.

"What's the condition of the *Mocking Bird's* crew?' the Captain asked.

They are attempting to regain control. They will not succeed.

Silence returned to the bridge as they flew on. They flew for the better part of a day before Mira's display finally picked up signs of life. It was nestled deep in the mountains and looked to be a camp of some sort. When they flew down into the valley and saw what it was, Josh's heart sank. The only sign of life on this planet that was supposed to be earth was able to fit into one camp that looked barely bigger than the *Raven* herself.

Is this all that's left? he asked himself. The *Mocking Bird* stayed in a hover as the *Raven* moved ahead to inspect the area. The ship's sensors said there was life, but it certainly did not look like it. The tents were ripped and beaten, surely useless against the elements, and flapped in the wind created by the *Raven's* engines. So far they hadn't seen any movement. The forest around the camp was blackened like every other forest they had seen, as if the trees had been burned, and areas that looked like they used to be gardens or crops were dug out and destroyed.

"I give you this, it was effective," Josh said to Mira. She just nodded in response.

The silence in the bridge was broken by an alarm. Mira instantly shifted her display, "Anti-aircraft weapon, locked on...missile in the air!"

Josh instinctively tighten his grip on the controls and pushed the *Raven* forward.

"Helm Master. Fall back, Weapons Master protect the *Mocking Bird.* There is no way she can fight in her current state," the Captain ordered.

Excellent thinking Captain. The creature praised.

There was no response from the Captain as Josh spun the *Raven* around bolting for the *Mocking Bird* which was climbing away from the engagement.

"Second missile inbound," Mira reported, "They aren't heading for the *Mocking Bird*."

"Alright Helm Master. Time to show them what we can do."

On board the *Mocking Bird*, Bridge

Date: July 24, 3000

Time: 22h00 zulu

Location: Unknown

Tanner nearly lost his footing as the *Mocking Bird* lurched upwards. The threat display lit up and an alarm sounded. When he looked out the window he could see the *Raven* being followed by two missiles. Although slower than lasers, the missiles would cause more damage even if they only hit the shields. Tanner smiled, maybe that ship wasn't getting away after all. Then the *Raven* pulled a maneuver that made his jaw go slack. It keeled up on one side and a wave of silver passed over the ship as its shields dropped. The missiles flew right between its engines, just barely missing the ship's flank and exploded harmlessly behind the *Raven*. The *Raven* then leveled out and another wave of silver signified its shields were active again. Tanner couldn't believe his eyes.

"One hell of a crew," he muttered to himself again. More explosions erupted as the *Raven* dealt with the anti-aircraft defense surrounding the underground base they had found. Tanner wondered if the *Raven's* crew knew the implications of what they were doing. By taking out the air defense the base was left open to attack by the creature that now was helping the *Raven* and her crew.

"What's the status on us regaining control?" Tanner asked.

"We aren't going to be able to. We are locked out of all controls," the First Officer reported.

Tanner shook his head and was about to respond when the *Mocking Bird* suddenly dove towards the *Raven*. It leveled out flying by her side down towards the base. Tanner swallowed hard. If the *Raven* kept to its word and returned the *Mocking Bird's* crew safely, then Tanner was a dead man walking. Ever since the war against the *Raven's* monster, the military hadn't taken kindly to failure. If he returned without the completion of his mission then he would be stripped of his commission and sent to survive in the wild on his own, or be killed on the spot. He actually preferred the second option. He was so deep in thought in how to avoid his fate that he didn't notice the crowd gathering on the base as they landed or the fact that the evacuation alarm had sounded. What did bring his attention back was a message.

Time to go Captain.

For some odd reason Tanner complied and followed his crew off. When Tanner disembarked he wasn't surprise to see his commanding officer, General Broke, waiting for him.

"Crew of the *Mocking Bird* reporting sir." Tanner saluted. He tried to stay the shaking in his voice. After all this time, the engagements against the enemy and the *Raven,* he had never truly been scared, but now he was terrified.

"You failed your mission I see." Brook's voice was ice cold.

"Sir we–"

"We do not accept failure," Brook said, and withdrew his side arm, "Congratulations First Officer, you've been promoted." Tanner braced himself for the shot. Sure enough, he heard the gun fire, but instead of the bullet tearing through his flesh he heard the sound of it hitting metal. When he opened his eyes, he saw that the *Mocking Bird* had repositioned herself so that one of her undamaged landing gear doors was down in a protective barrier between Tanner and General Brook.

It saved me? Tanner questioned. Before he could do anything the door moved forward, knocking the General to the ground. Tanner watch in fascinated horror as one of the *Mocking Bird's* guns raked the General's body. Instantly the base's guards began to fire back. The *Mocking Bird* positioned herself so she was between the bullets and her crew, while the *Raven* circled around behind.

"What are they doing sir?" the First Officer asked. Tanner studied the *Mocking Bird* closely. It wasn't being calculating as the other creature he had seen had been. It had wasted ammunition on the General when one bullet would have achieved the desired result. No, the ship was acting irrationally.

"It's protecting us," Tanner replied not fully believing his own words. The *Mocking Bird* was not discriminating in its targets. If it moved she shot it. The way it was moving made Tanner realize something.

It's almost as though it is shooting in rage, he thought to himself. Sure enough, even after the bullets stopped flying, the *Mocking Bird* seemed to be almost panting in anger. The *Raven* hovered in front of the *Mocking Bird.* The two ships stayed in a hover, the *Raven*'s position preventing the *Mocking Bird* from inflicting more damage to the base. They stayed like that for many minutes as a seemingly voiceless conversation calmed the *Mocking Bird* down. The *Raven* then positioned herself next to the *Mocking Bird* and they climbed away from the base. All the while the *Mocking Bird* had guns trained on anything that might be a threat to her crew.

"Amazing," Tanner whispered and the ships disappeared behind the mountains.

On board the *Raven*, Bridge

Date: July 26, 3000

Time: 10h00 zulu

Location: Unknown

Josh stifled a yawn as he watched the instruments. The crew had become reconciled to the sight of a blackened world and was ready to leave. The problem was that the *Mocking Bird* wasn't. They had been hiding behind the mountains surrounding the base for a little over a day. Each attempt to move resulted in the *Mocking Bird* refusing. It wanted to make sure it's crew was safe. As far as Josh could tell, this was the case. But they stayed none the less.

"Alright, this is getting ridiculous," the First Officer piped up, "Captain, how long are we going to sit here?"

"The *Mocking Bird* is our only way home, and if it won't leave, neither do we," the Captain responded evenly.

"Can't the Weapons Master just threaten to shoot it?" the First Officer asked.

That would be a bad idea.

The Captain readjusted himself in his seat, "Why?"

There was no response from the creature till Josh asked the same question,

The *Mocking Bird* and I are intelligent life forms. If we feel threatened we react much like any of your wild animals. Fight or flight instinct I believe you call it. Only we don't run. We eliminate the threat. If the *Raven* becomes a threat, she has no need for us and she will fight back, despite her injuries.

"Don't you control the *Mocking Brid*?" Mira inquired.

Yes and no. I have no more control over her then your Captain does you. Under normal conditions she would follow my orders without question. The problem is we have never had to deal with the certain emotions we face now.

"Like what?" Josh asked.

Dedication. Responsibility. We've only ever had to survive. Now though, we have crews. The *Mocking Bird* has left hers behind and now wants to make sure they are cared for. Additionally, she knows we can't leave without her and will exploit this.

Josh let his mind play over what he was reading. It made sense. They weren't human so why would their emotional conditions be the same. It would also explain the reaction of the Rook impersonator to the sight of the world he created in the future. The two ships were becoming human, and couldn't handle it.

"Then we wait," the Captain concluded.

The bridge went silent till Josh thought of something, "Sir, if I may?"

"Yes Helm Master. What is it?"

Josh swallowed, not sure if this was a good idea, "Who did she bond with?"

The Captain raised an eye brow, "Pardon?"

"Our creature has seemed to have bonded with me. Maybe the *Mocking Bird* bonded with one of her crew and won't leave them behind."

It is possible. But unlikely.

"Why would it be unlikely," the Captain asked.

I found the Helm Master to be key to my survival and still do. He nearly died trying to defend you and his ship. I found it admirable, and as I now know was a sign of his loyalty. The *Mocking Bird* has never been exposed to such events.

"She saved their Captain," the First Officer pointed out.

"Sir. I noticed the *Mocking Bird's* accuracy with her weapons. Could it be possible it might relate to the Weapons Master?" the First Officer proposed.

The Captain remained silent, evidently pondering the possibility, "Patch her through, will you?"

Again, no response from the *Raven*.

"Do as he say," Josh ordered

Very well.

Within seconds a message appeared on Mira's display,

Who are you?

Mira looked to Josh, "Just talk to it like it's a person," Josh prompted.

Mira nodded, "I am the Weapons Master on board the *Raven*."

The Raven has told me about you. You seem to have an affiliation with the one the *Raven* favors.

Josh was thankful that the message was only visible to him and Mira. Mira, however, ignored the implications, "*Mocking Bird*, we need to leave now. Your crew is home. There is nothing to be gained by staying." Mira's voice had taken a stricter tone.

We will stay until I am satisfied.

"Try ordering her," Josh encouraged. He could tell the Captain wasn't too pleased with having the *Raven* under the control of something that wouldn't take his orders and even less so of the fact that both ships would likely ignore him. But they did have to get home.

"You will leave now," Mira ordered.

No. *The Mocking Bird* replied like a stubborn teenager.

"Yes. Now. You will follow and you will not protest or I will take action."

Josh winced, that might show them as a threat.

Such as?

"We made those marks on your side. We'll do it again." Mira threatened.

Weapons Master. You may be doing more harm than good. The ship cautioned.

"I agree Weapons Master," the Captain said. Josh said nothing; he waited for the reply.

Very well. I am in no condition to fight.

The bridge let out a collective sigh of relief and Josh began to lead them away from the mountains. A couple of hours later they were in the Time Stream for what was hopefully their last time.

On board the *Raven*; Bridge

Date: Unknown

Time: Unknown

Location: Unknown

Josh looked to the Captain for the order. This was it; they would be home after this exit. Now the ships just needed a break in the tunnel to exit through. Josh scanned the walls looking for a less violent place. Naturally the area they wanted to get through seemed to be one of the most violent walls Josh had seen this entire mission. Finally, he spotted an exit point and the two ships crashed through, literally. There was a blazing flash of purple light and it looked as though the *Raven* tore part of the Time Stream with it as it exited. That fact was lost though as the ship was sent into a flat spin. Josh fought with the controls. He noted the *Mocking Bird* in a dive, from which she quickly recovered. It began to fly a circuit around the spinning *Raven*. Josh worked the engine pitch controls to try and level the ship out but quickly realized that it was no use. The engines had jammed in the Time Stream flight position. They would never supply the lift needed to get out of this maneuver.

"Force the engines forward," Josh ordered the ship as he grappled to try and right the spin.

It may damage the internal components.

"If you don't we'll hit the ground!" Josh snapped back. The sound of grinding gears made Josh cringe as the wings were forced forward. Just a fraction of a second before the *Raven* plowed into the water below it stopped falling, Josh managed to keep her in a hover just above the water. A mist sprayed up by the four massive engines flew around the ship. Josh let out a sigh of relief. They were over an ocean, to their left was a coast line, to the right nothing but wide-open space.

"Are we in the right place?" the Captain asked.

"Based on the reading, we are home sir," the First Officer reported. The crew erupted into cheers.

This is not what I expected.

"You saw 1970. Why would this be any different?"

I never thought that was your realm. Particularly not after having seen where the *Mocking Bird* came from.

"Welcome to earth, my time." Josh replied, laughing at how stupid it sounded. Josh felt a hand on his arm and turned to see Mira smiling.

"You did it. You got us home."

Josh smiled. He had done it. He had disappointed the Captain, and himself, but they were home, and alive.

It is remarkable, even the water seems pure.

Mira stifled a laughed, "You know I could get used to you *Raven*."

And I you Weapons Master. Take care of the Helm Master, will you? The message displayed solely on Mira's displays.

At that moment, the *Mocking Bird* passed in front of them, the force of her engines sending a wave crashing down on the *Raven*. Everyone watched as the massive ship climbed, rolled and swung around for another pass.

This should be, how you say, fun, the *Raven's* creature said seconds before all the displays went black.

Josh was about to question it when the ship spun around and managed to splash a huge wave on the *Mocking Bird's* flank as it passed by.

The Captain raised an eyebrow, "Helm Master?"

"Was not me, sir," Josh responded.

"We are locked out again," the First Officer reported as the *Raven* shot forward chasing after the *Mocking Bird*.

"What's going on?" the Captain asked, the agitation clear in his voice.

Josh and Mira traded glances.

"They're playing, sir," Mira stated.

On board the *Raven*; Bridge

Date: January 12, 2029

Time: 13h00 Zulu

Location: 36.738121°N, 75.958726°W

Having successfully coaxed the *Raven* and the *Mocking Bird* out of their water fight, Josh and Mira had directed them toward the *Raven's* home base. Josh could feel the Captain's growing dislike for the idea of his own ship, and another, being under the command of someone lower in the chain of command. Not that he blamed him of course. It would certainly raise a red flag for him as well, even without the attempted assassination.

What surprised Josh was how close the *Mocking Bird* and Mira seemed to be. They were constantly talking with each other throughout the flight, mostly on what earth was like. From the little Josh had learned of from the creature inside the *Raven*, the world it came from was a planet covered in contaminated water with an extravagant underground tunnel system where they resided as the alpha predator.

What brought you first into the Time Stream?

The message on Josh's display broke his train of thought. The reason seemed so silly to Josh now. Seeing what destruction could lay ahead, and what other worlds could be like, almost sickened him.

"Research, on the implication of time travel as a weapon in war," Josh replied.

I knew that from my files. I wanted to know why you personally came. It seems a great risk, and at the time the Weapons Master was not in the picture to persuade your judgement.

Josh sighed. He wasn't entirely sure of the reason himself. He just knew he had come, and that he was going to do a good job. "I suppose it was to make a difference."

By aiding in creating a weapon of war?

"Yes and no. I was in the military before I was put on the Time project. I thought if we had access to time travel that it would allow us to dissolve conflict before it began, hopefully resulting in world peace," Josh explained.

"That, and you wanted to fly the big cool plane," Mira teased.

A noble cause Helm Master, *Mocking Bird*'s message read.

Indeed. Even if it was naïve.

"Either way we followed our orders. Now we know not to try that again."

Your species will try again. They made me after all. They will try to take advantage of your discoveries and data that you collected. It will lead to the navigation system I have onboard and also the ability to have more controlled exits than you're...

The *Mocking Bird* left the statement unfinished as Josh chuckled, "You're probably right. But I don't want to think of that now."

You will not be returning as a Helm Master?

Josh was about to say he would return as the *Raven's* Helm Master before he remembered something. He had agreed to help this thing get home. The creature had trusted him to do that, but if they landed there was no way that was going to happen. He felt a frown slip onto his face.

"How are we getting you home?" Josh mumbled.

I thought this was your home *Raven*, the *Mocking Bird* said.

Worry not on the matter Helm Master. I will stay and continue to serve under you. I need not return to from where I came. It would cause further complications for you and the rest of the crew.

I believe I will stay under the command of the Weapons Master as well.

Josh and Mira exchanged glances. Mira was the first to speak, "I don't know what will happen to you guys, or us for that matter."

Josh ran a hand over the controls, "It is very possible that the *Raven* will be put back into service and updated but as for the *Mocking Bird*...It's heavily damaged. I don't know if they will do much more then use you for research."

I'll heal.

There was no farther communication among the four as they approached the base. It was relatively simple to get clearance to land. The Captain had to do some explaining as to why they had an additional aircraft but soon they were hovering over the respective landing areas. Much to Josh's surprise landing gear extended from the *Mocking Brid's* belly and she set down gracefully. Josh lowered the *Raven* to the tarmac setting it down gently. No one on the bridge spoke as they went about shutting the *Raven* down. Josh reached for the engine controls and found them held in place. A message from the creature provided an explanation,

I can't let you do that. The Mocking Bird and I survive off their energy.

Josh, for whatever reason, didn't question it, "Very well. Thank you for your help...uhm...Rook?"

Please call me *Raven*. Rook was a form of me that caused you nothing but pain and suffering.

"Well then *Raven*, I was wrong; neither of you are truly monsters," Mira said from her seat.

Take care Weapons Master.

"Helm Master, are we clear to disembark?" the Captain asked. It was a normal question but it took Josh a couple of seconds to respond. He quickly worked the controls, thankfully the *Raven's* engine design allowed the cores to remain running while the engines omitted no thrust making it safe for people to approach the vessel.

"Yes sir. All systems locked and clear," Josh reported.

The Captain nodded, "Well, what are you waiting for. Let's get our debriefing over with so you can all go see your families, you are all dismissed." The bridge crew wasted no time leaving. Josh, Mira and the Captain were the last ones left when a message on the main display grabbed their attention.

Captain,I apologize for my transgression towards you. After having accessed various resources on the networks around this base I now understand the importance of strong

leadership in order bring the most from a team. You have clearly done an excellent job.

"Thank you," the Captain said simply, "Helm Master, Weapons Master. I hope you will understand the importance of discretion?" Josh looked to Mira. Was the Captain giving them a free pass for when he had caught them the other day? Or was it week? Josh had long ago lost track of days, he wasn't even sure how long they had been gone despite it being their scheduled return date. "Are you ready to leave your post?"

Mira stood to leave, "You coming?"

Josh nodded, "Yah. Thanks again *Raven*. I look forward to flying again with you."

Goodbye Helm Master.

With that Josh leaned on Mira and the Captain as they slowly made their way out of the ship onto the tarmac, keeping Josh's wounds in mind.

Josh had no one waiting for him, despite the crowd around the two massive time traveling aircrafts. Josh surveyed the scene. It looked as though the entire base was outside to see their arrival. It was almost peaceful and more than a welcome sight for him. A group of men with quite a few bars on each sleeve rushed to them.

"Captain Anderson!" the Base Commander called excitedly. "Did you do it? Did you get the data?"

"I believe we did but unfortunately the *Raven* needs a lot of work before it can return to the Time Stream." The Captain explained.

"I don't understand."

"We got lost," Josh interjected.

The Base Commander looked to Josh. He eyed him carefully, "Pardon?"

"The navigation system didn't have the processing power to deal with the complexity of the Time Stream," The Captain explained, "It failed as soon as we entered. If not for my Helm Master and Weapons Master, we would still be lost."

"But you're on time," the Base Commander remarked.

Josh couldn't help but roll his eyes, *Right. A time machine, late.*

"What happened to your crew," the Deputy Base Commander asked, motioning to Josh.

"That's a complicated story," the Captain began. "I will provide a detailed report but we had some minor engagements in our mission."

Mira let out a laugh, "Minor doesn't begin to describe what that thing did to us."

The Commander seemed willing to forgive Josh's and Mira's outburst and ready to move on to more questions when a large gust of wind nearly blew them all over. Dust and debris flew at the crowd as everyone turned to see the *Raven* and *Mocking Bird* taking to the sky.

"What's happening, Anderson?" the Base Commander shouted over the engine noise.

So that's their plan. Get us off and fly home, Josh thought, *just like we did with the Mocking Bird's crew.* He smiled, *fitting.* Then the two ships did something that he didn't expect. They fired their weapons. The large laser blast leveled the hangar and research building on the base and the following blast would surely have destroyed the underground part of the base. The two ships were destroying everything the project had, and unwittingly killing everyone left inside the research center. If that happened it meant the all the data, design plans and all, would be gone, leaving the only valuable information left of the project that took years of work—the data collected and stored on the *Raven*—and that was about to fly away. Josh couldn't believe it as he watched the two ships flew off.

"Anderson, order your crew to stand down!" The Base Commander yelled.

"There are no crew left on board to order!" Anderson called back.

Then the *Mocking Bird* erupted into a blinding flash of light as it disintegrated. The crowd quickly ran for what cover there was. No one but the higher ranks, the Captain, First Officer, Josh and Mira stayed, watching as the obliterated *Mocking Brid* burned in the sky.

"Are they doing what I think they're doing?" Mira asked. Josh nodded. He watched the *Raven* fly up high. It was big enough he could still make out the individual engines. If he was right she wouldn't stay flying longer. The *Raven* did a few rolls and tricks before it leveled out. It did a low fly by, tipping its wings to the Helm and Weapons Master before climbing back up again. Then the *Raven's* self-destruct activated. All four of the engines detonated, their plasma cores causing a huge fire ball that engulfed the *Raven* as the plasma ate away at her frame. It fell breaking and twisting painfully through the air before it was completely dissolved. Not a single of piece of the aircraft hit the ground. Josh stood stunned. His ship was gone, destroyed, with nothing left.

"What is the meaning of this!" The Deputy Base Commander hollered to the Captain.

The Captain saluted the streaks of smoke in the sky before responding, "They may have just saved us from our own fate."

Acknowledgments

I would like to acknowledge the contributions of Sharyn Heagle who provided moral and technical support along with knowledge to which I would not otherwise have had access. Without her, this book would not have been possible. Thank you to my mother Betty Gloutney and to Melody Tomka for their assistance in editing this manuscript. Finally, thanks to my family and friends who stood behind me and put up with the process of my writing this manuscript. Thanks to you all.

Born in Amherst Nova Scotia, Patrick Gloutney moved to Ottawa in 2012 where he pursued his education and career in Aviation. As an active member of the local flying community, he has been the recipient of awards ranging from community involvement to safety and professionalism including the Rockcliffe Flying Club's Ken Chatfield Memorial Trophy for his dedication, enthusiasm, camaraderie, and professionalism in the local flying community. When is not working as a pilot and contributing to the development of his flying community Patrick continues to explore many different avenues in his writing career producing a wide variety of written work.

http://www.patrickgloutney.simplesite.com

www.ingramcontent.com/pod-product-compliance
Lightning Source LLC
Chambersburg PA
CBHW021919170626
46807CB00007B/2889

* 9 7 8 0 9 9 4 7 2 5 1 5 8 *